BE
MORE
CHILL

Also by Ned Vizzini

It's Kind of a Funny Story

BE
MORE
CHILL

NED VIZZINI

HYPERION

LOS ANGELES   NEW YORK

Text copyright © 2004 by Ned Vizzini
Afterword copyright © 2015 by David Levithan

Printed in the United States of America
First Hardcover Edition, June 2004
First Paperback Edition, September 2005
15 14 13 12
FAC-025438-18187

Library of Congress Control Number for Hardcover: 2003057086
ISBN 978-0-7868-0996-7

Visit www.hyperionteens.com

TO:

Naomi (very much the most important: hi, babe),
Samartha, Bridget, Kate, Carrie, Jessica, Samantha,
Effy, Other Kate, That Girl I Hung Out with in
Prospect Park, That Spanish Girl from Karaoke,
Karla, Sarah, Claudia, Elyssa (Wilin' Chick), Olga,
Lai Sze, Nicole (Bracey), Katia, Vanessa, Heavenly,
and Those Other Girls at New Year's Eve 2001
(including Ursula), That Girl from Nice Guy
Eddie's, Caroline, Alina Who Ended up with a Guy
Named Dogshit, Anna, Marnie, Other Caroline,
Robyn, and Chelsea

PART 1
pre-squip

one

The room is bright and alive at 8:45 A.M.—I can almost ignore Middle Borough High School's zombie fluorescent lighting. Mr. Gretch is up at his desk, a tall bald head with wisps of hair and a beard. He's accompanied by a newspaper and a cactus; in about twenty seconds he's going to take attendance. To my left is Jenna Rolan, the Coolest girl in class.

Jenna is already talking: "She was like, 'I'll only do it if you beat me in pool!' And then of course she intentionally lost in pool. What a slut!"

Jenna likes to talk about her friend Elizabeth, who is a "real" slut. In fact, when I think about it, Jenna never talks about her family, or TV, or when work is due, or the ins and outs of procuring concert tickets, like most girls. She just talks about how Elizabeth is a slut.

"You should've seen what she was wearing. It was like a garbage bag with a condom on top—"

"Bwer-her-her!" Anne laughs. Anne is the second-Coolest girl in the class, which is math. She sits in front of me so she's always twisting back in her chair to talk to Jenna, which reinforces the fact that Jenna is Coolest and she is second-Coolest. Girls are very territorial.

"Ka-yur-uhhhh." Mr. Gretch clears his throat from the front of the room. "Abbey."

"Here."

"Asu."

"Here."

"Atborough."

"Here."

"Azu, not-Asu." Mr. Gretch absentmindedly cups his cactus. This never seems to hurt him.

"Here."

"Caniglia."

Christine raises her hand. I look over at her. She looks beautiful. "Here." I look down.

"Duvoknovich."

"Here."

"Goranski."

"Here."

"Heere?"

Oh yeah.

Here comes the fun part, the part that has been stressing me since they started taking attendance (in fifth grade). I can't say "here" in response to my name. It confuses teachers. I raise my hand quietly and say: "Present." Somebody snickers up by the front of the room. Are they snickering at me? Are they? Can never be too sure. I pull out one of my preprinted Humiliation Sheets, write the date up top and put a tally mark next to the Snicker category. I cover the page tightly so Jenna can't see. Then I re-tune my ears to listen for copycat snickering.

two

The Humiliation Sheets have developed a lot over the years, with a host of different categories, but the current model has Snicker, Laugh, Snotty Comment, Refusal to Return a Head Nod (the standard form of greeting at Middle Borough High), Refusal to Return a Verbal Greeting, Refusal to Touch Hands, Public Denial of Formerly Agreed-Upon Opinion, Refusal to Repeat a Joke, and Mortification Event (a catch-all). I use the Humiliation Sheets to keep track of my social status in a concrete, quantitative way. They are my secret, totally; I make sure no one sees them as I fill them up with tally marks every day. I hate tally marks.

Up in front, Mr. Gretch writes k on the board—k sucks in math; once you see it you might as well ignore everything and save yourself. Mr. Gretch can't hear on account of he's, well, *old*, so Jenna keeps talking and I keep listening.

"Okay and then Elizabeth was like, 'Where can we go? I don't have a car like you.' . . . And the guy says"—Jenna puts on a low voice—" 'Come and sit on this pipe, babe.' And she went! Unbe*liev*able."

Anne eats it up—*"Bwer-her-her"*—craning her neck to suck in every word. It's far enough into the school year—mid-October—for kids to have stopped talking about summer. (The big story was that Jake Dillinger had sex with this model from Czechoslovakia who was dating his dad, which I believe. Jake can do anything.) Mostly people are talking about the parties of the past weekend or the PSATs, which are coming up. There's also scattered chatter about the Halloween Dance.

"I hear Brianna has, like, five boys lined up? Because with football players, you don't know if one of them is going to sprain his ankle and not be able to dance?" Anne uptalks.

Jenna gives back cold silence. "That happened to me in junior high. My then-boyfriend broke his leg and I had to dance with him while he was on crutches and a cast and it was *so horrible.*"

I tune my ears from Jenna–Anne to other pockets of activity in the room. Mark Jackson and this other kid—his name is actually Jackson Marks—discuss video games. Rob works out a math problem, probably something post-calculus, while picking at his mouth, ear, and nose as if he has them on shuffle.

Barbary explains how everyone has to call him "Dr. Barbary" now because he ordered a Ph.D. off the Internet. And Christine, quiet in her invisible pod up by the front of the room, just looks pretty.

"Ooh, I heard Christine Caniglia has a new stalker," Jenna says.

Whoa!

"Jenna!" Anne whispers like she's protecting something. "He's right *there*!"

Double whoa. I sit quietly, stiff. Calm. Calm. My head is turned so they must not think I'm listening, but I'm always listening. I'm wired. I peek at Jenna. She eyes me as if I'm a mildly interesting object between her and the clock. I turn back.

"Yeah, that's him," she says to Anne. "I heard he wrote her a letter."

I never wrote any letter! I never even *said* anything to Christine, not once, except, "Don't press C7, the Nutri-Grain bars get stuck in this machine," that one time out by the Student Union office where the Nutri-Grain bars get stuck in the machine, because I can't talk to Christine. I just look at her and think about her a lot because she's beautiful, you know? I mean she's intelligent and sweet and everything else that a girl is supposed to be to offset her beauty, but even if she were idiotic and mean, she'd still be beautiful and I'd still be contorted.

"He *is* weird," Jenna says.

This is a bad day for me to start hearing this stuff. In my pocket is a Shakespeare made of chocolate, okay, like one of those Easter bunny chocolates, but in the shape of Shakespeare, and I was going to give it to Christine today at our first play rehearsal. I clutch it.

Jenna whispers something I can't quite catch. I slide my elbow across my Humiliation Sheet and put a tally mark under Mortification Event, because I don't have a specific category for people whispering about me. I should. Just then Mr. Gretch does the stupid classic high-school move and I can't even believe it's being done to me: "And Jeremy, can you tell us what that angle would be?"

My notebook isn't open. It's being used as a Humiliation Sheet shield. My neurons aren't depolarizing. (I learned that in bio.)

Mortification Event number two.

three

At lunch I seek out my best friend Michael Mell. Michael sits in a different place in the cafeteria every day—sometimes the indoor part with the long Formica tables, sometimes the outdoor part with the scarred picnic benches and giant bees—but you can always spot him because he's a tall white boy with a white-boy afro and *huge* headphones. They have a cord coming off them that's spiraled like an old phone cord. The headphones let him plunk down anywhere, with the jocks or Warhammer nerds or at one of the girl tables (although Michael only sits with Asian girls). No one bothers him when he has them on because he's obviously got important things on his mind.

"What's up?" I say as I approach. Michael doesn't listen to a thing in those headphones during lunch. He just likes how they feel on his head.

"*Mmmmgph,*" he says, wolfing down a fish-patty sandwich with cheese and chocolate milk. "'Sup?"

"Big problems," I say.

I pull the chocolate Shakespeare out of my pocket (it's wrapped in Victorian era–style foil), plop it on the table, and prop my elbows up to either side of it. "I don't think I can give this to Christine."

"*Mmmmrrrr*, yuh."

"Michael."

"Yuh."

"You want to finish that?"

Michael smiles and lets chewed fish-cheese roll through the gap in his teeth. It plats onto the tray in front of him.

"Crackhead," I laugh. "People are going to see you."

"Uh-nuh," Michael says; his Adam's apple bobs up and down as his food slides away. "Yeah, so, ah," he drinks milk, wipes his mouth on the back of his wrist. "What's with Christine? You pussying out?"

"Yeah, well." I haven't touched my food. "It's bad."

"What's bad? I totally know how it is. Did you say something dumb to her?"

"Well, no, but people *think* I did. Which is basically the same thing."

"No," Michael says, working on an orange ice cream bar now. "You doing something and people *thinking* that you did it are actually really different."

"Well, people *think* I gave her a letter."

Michael's body rocks. He grins: "'I've got your

You've got my song—'" I punch him in the
...der. "Ow!"

...No Weezer, okay?"

"I'll try." Michael folds his hands. "So who *thinks*
you wrote Christine a letter?"

"Jenna Rolan. She also said I was her 'new
stalker.'"

"You're such a girl." Michael gets up and slides his
tray into a nearby garbage can. "So what? Does
Christine care? That's who's important, right?"

"Yeah, she's who's important, but she's not the
only thing that matters in this whole . . . situation,"
I say, making circles with my hands to emphasize
situation. "It's like, do I still give this to her or not?
Will it seem too stalkerish?"

"Jeremy." Michael fixes buttons on his shirt.
"That chocolate Shakespeare is genius. She's gonna
love chocolate, because everybody does, except for
those weird people who only like chips"—Michael
glances one table away at a red-headed girl eating
chips—"and she's in a Shakespeare play with you, so
obviously she's gonna like Shakespeare."

"But what if she thinks I'm an obsessed loser?" I
start in on the bean salad on my tray. It came cold
but feels colder.

"Dude," Michael says. "Think of how you'll feel if
you *don't* give it to her. Think of how you'll feel at
home tonight, jerking off, having missed your chance."

"Oh yeah. Well, duh, I'll feel like . . ." Like I do all the time, like I feel whenever I can't dial a phone number or dance at a dance or hold a hand right. Like I'm used to feeling. "Like shit."

"Right, so give it to her—"

"Yo, tall-ass, could you maybe sit or move from the garbage can?" Rich says to Michael. Rich has come on the scene; that's what he does best. He's shorter than us but very built. He has blond hair with a streak of red in the back, like a rooster. Michael moves aside and Rich dumps his whole tray, including the actual tray, into the trash. He eyes us.

"What? Punks."

four

At the end of the day I walk Middle Borough's elongated and well-painted hall—my school has one giant hallway that you enter in the middle of, so the whole place is like the Great Wall of Metuchen, New Jersey, with the echoes of the swim team at one end and the sound of the theater door opening and closing at the other end, where I'm going.

So far, in high school (I too have an extensive middle-school career), I've been in *The Tempest* and *You're a Good Man, Charlie Brown* to rave reviews, both times, from my mom. I like everything about school plays—being at school after school, learning my lines in the bathroom, how the performance always seems totally screwed up a week before it goes on, but then comes together at the last minute, how the second show always manages to be better than the first, how everyone takes their bow at the end and the parents are standing, showing off their digital camcorders, and your costume is hot, but you figure, okay, that's the price of my art and then— Bam! Cast party! I love cast parties. I've never been to one, actually, truthfully, but I'm sure they're great.

"Hey, you're in this play?" I ask Mark Jackson from math as I sit down next to him. Mark's my friend, sort of.

"Yeah, I'm in this dilly deal," he says. He's playing Game Boy SP. "What's it called again?"

"A Midsummer Night's Dream," I say. "You don't even know the name of your own play?" Only I don't say that.

"Midsummer Night's Drizz-eem. Gotcha."

I sit down two places from him in a seat that looks like it was stained with condom residue—not that I would know, except for that one time in my room when I was messing around with one to see what it would look like in the mirror—

"Hot. Hot to death," Mark says.

"What?"

"I'm talking to the game, yo. Mind your beeswax."

I look over at Mark's game, or, uh, "beeswax," as the case might be. It looks like he's driving an SUV on underground train tracks shooting a high-powered rifle at homeless people.

"No peeking, dorkus malorkus," Mark says, snatching his Game Boy away, imperiling his driving and shooting. "I'm the only one in the school with KAP Three; you gotta pay me five bucks to look at it."

"What's KAP Three?"

"Kill All People. Three."

"Uh . . ."

"You never heard of Kill All People? What's *wrong* with you?" Mark eyes me. I sit silent, keeping my head and mouth steady, staring ahead. After a few seconds, Marks slides down a seat, like I have herpes. (Or lupus, right? Lupus.) Then I move down a row.

"Fuck, Jeremy, you don't have to be such a bitch," he remarks as I take my new seat. Just then Christine, uncharacteristically late for something, walks down the aisle past us. She rolls her eyes at Mark and while she's doing it, it is possible that they land on my person for a millisecond or two. Wow. When's the teacher getting here?

"Aaaaaaaaaaaaa!" Mr. Reyes shrieks from the entrance to the theater. *"Mwaaaaaaaa!* Greetings all! I'm not sure you realize it, but I have a very powerful falsetto voice! *Baaaaaaaaaaaa!"*

"Damn, this dude is fruit-aliciously homo-rific," Mark says behind me. Little digital homeless people groan as they die on his Game Boy SP.

"It is wonderful to see you here!" Mr. Reyes gets on stage behind a mic, which he does not need. "I am glad to have such a captive audience for my voice. *Laaaaaaaaa!* I am also very glad to have such a wonderful cast; we are going to have a great time in the play." Mr. Reyes is tall and skinny with no facial hair; he wears a suit and tie. He teaches English for his day job.

"So let's see who's here, and I will give you all your parts. Jeremy Heere!"

"Yes." I get up.

"There's no need to stand. You must simply know that you have gotten the role of Lysander. This is a very demanding role that will take much of your time."

"Thank you, Mr. Reyes."

"Jake?"

Jake Dillinger is in this play too? Guess it isn't enough to be on the football team and nail a Czechoslovakian model and be a leader in the SU. Down in front, he shifts in his seat slightly to acknowledge Mr. Reyes.

"You are going to be Demetrius, another tough role. Get ready to memorize much-ly."

"Cool," Jake says.

"Puck? Where is my Puck? Christine Caniglia?"

Christine is now down in front, near Jake; all I see is her blond hair.

"You're kidding!" she squirts. "I'm *Puck*?"

"You, young lady, are Puck."

"Yes!" Christine jumps out of her seat, pumping her fist. Everyone eyes her with respect and swelled-up cutesy pride, or maybe that's just me;

when girls get happy and jump out of their seats, like on *The Price Is Right*, it's sweet to watch.

"Don't get too excited, Christine; it's a disgusting number of lines. *Maaaaaaah!*" Mr. Reyes moves on through Hermia, Helena, Titania, Bottom, and about a dozen other people. Mark, behind me with his Game Boy, gets to be some kind of cross-dressing elf. That's comforting.

"Okay, those are the roles; now we must have the read-through. Ladies, fetch two metal chairs each and bring them on stage."

"Wuh?" The girls down in front look confused. (It's funny how they look confused from behind, with their shoulders bunched up.) Christine is the only one I hear: "How come we have to get the chairs?"

"Come come, it's a trade-off each time," Mr. Reyes says. "The men will be on chair-fetching tomorrow. Speaking of which, men! Pick a representative to go to the Teachers' Lounge and have them microwave my Hot Pocket!"

"For the whole play?" I ask. I don't want to get stuck with *that* job.

"No, Jeremy, just for today. Next time the girls will pick someone to go."

"I don't understand," Mark says behind me, actually pausing KAP Three. "Could you explain that again, please?"

"*Huggggh,*" Mr. Reyes says. "On day one the girls

will set up the chairs and the *guys* will pick a representative to get my Hot Pocket; on day two the guys will set up the chairs and the *girls* will pick a representative to get my Hot Pocket; then it repeats. . . . Does anyone have a question about this?"

Yes, of course: someone up front has one, and another, and another. When we finally get it all sorted out, this kid Jonah with a lisp fetches the Hot Pocket as the girls lug furniture, and then Mr. Reyes brings us on stage, where we sit in a circle of chairs (the girls made it a bit small) as if it were time for Duck-Duck-Goose, but really it's a read-through of *A Midsummer Night's Dream*, and really I'm not a little kid; I'm in high school. I have to remember that.

five

I grab the seat next to Christine's in the circle.

"So, uh, congratulations," I say quietly, speaking to the air in front of me and hoping she'll notice, "on Puck."

"What *is* this crap?" she turns, fierce. Christine has brown eyes with her blond hair. Up close she looks like all the cutest movie starlets, all those ones who haven't really been in any movies, but you see them in *Stuff* magazine or wherever, all combined in Photoshop, except that someone checked the Constrain Proportions box so nothing got distorted. "I can't believe he's making us *fetch* him chairs—isn't that illegal?"

"Uh, I don't think so, actually, but it's very bad—"

"Oh yeah, whatever. We don't have any rights under the Constitution about discrimination?"

"We don't have any rights under the Constitution at all, because we're students—"

"That is such crap!"

"Yeah . . ." I drum the head of Shakespeare in my pocket. "I'm Jeremy, by the way." I reach out to shake her hand, then pull back—I don't want people seeing.

"I know who you are," Christine says. "You're in my math, right?"

"Oh yeah." I pretend I wasn't aware of that fact. "But you know, you can be in a class with someone for a long time and never really—"

"Lysander!" Mr. Reyes snaps. "Speak!"

"Uh . . ." I'm Lysander, right?

"I'm Lysander, right?"

Mr. Reyes: "Yes."

"Yes. Okay, um . . . 'You have her father's love, Demetrius; Let me have Hermia's: do you marry him.'"

Mr. Reyes: "Thank you, Jeremy." He sucks in his lips in the angry/disappointed adult way. "Really excellent."

Me: "'Uh, I am, my Lord, as well derived as he, as well possessed—'"

Christine: "I hate him. His English classes are awful. He can't teach—"

Me: "'And, which is more than all these boasts can be I am beloved of beauteous—'"

Christine: "I'm seriously thinking about writing a letter about him to the *Metuchen Home News/Tribune*—"

I can't tell if Christine likes me or she just hates Mr. Reyes, but one way or another she's talking, and you can't beat that. I keep going, and every time I come to a sweet line in the read-through (and you know Shakespeare—the sweet lines are really sweet), I direct it at her, tilting my head so my sound waves ruffle some molecules on her cheek and she reacts in some imperceptible way that I might be imagining.

See, when I'm talking to girls, I develop an out-of-body consciousness, or unconsciousness. Everything means so much more. My posture, which is hopeless, gets a temporary lift as I arch my back. I can feel all my organs stacked in place and eyeball with pinpoint accuracy how far Christine's leg is from mine, and when they touch just for a second I wonder if it's her doing or my doing or chance. How can she *not* notice if our legs touch? How can she not notice my extremely unslick peripheral vision? How can she not notice my white socks, showing between my pants and shoes? (I have to fix that.)

"Lysander!" Mr. Reyes snaps again halfway though some scene with fairies. I scramble with the script. Christine smiles, which doesn't help me, and I try to smile back even though she might not be smiling at me, or she might be smiling at me in the wrong way, the eunuch way.

This is good. This is a step.

six

"'Give me your hands, if we be friends, And Robin shall restore amends,'" Christine reads. The end of *A Midsummer Night's Dream* is empty without applause. It's 5:30 and I'm sweaty in bad places.

"*Reagggggh . . .*" The cast collectively stretches, inching our chairs back. Some people have left during the reading, but there are still a dozen of us in the circle, including a napping Mr. Reyes.

"Right, hmmmm," he wakes up. "So that's the play. Tomorrow we're going to do scenes with Lysander and Demetrius. *Maaaaaaaaa!* We need everybody here, and *blah blah blah*—"

Scraping, chatting, yawning, we drown him in the dive for our backpacks. Here's my last chance to talk with Christine. I've got to (1) give her the chocolate Shakespeare and (2) be slick about it—like I'm her friend, but I could be more—and (3) leave the theater with a *flourish*.

"So, um, Christine," I manage before she gets off stage, talking to the back of her head. In my left pocket, a fist clenches and unclenches. In my right, Shakespeare stands tall. "Did you hear anything about me, ah, giving you a letter?"

"Mm?" She faces me. That doesn't sound like a good *Mm*.

"A letter, like . . . Well, in my math class this morning Jenna, who sits next to me, y'know, Jenna Rolan, said something about me giving you a letter, and, like, I don't even know you that well, so there might be, or have been, a misunderstanding."

"I don't understand."

I don't either, and that's what I just said. Doesn't she know what a misunderstanding is? I don't say anything.

"You want to make sure that you *didn't* give me a letter?"

"Well . . ."

"Why? What's this about?" Christine leans her folding chair against her hip.

"Well, I just hate when rumors get started because they're really hurtful, you know, and—"

"You didn't, okay?"

"Okay."

"You didn't give me any letter. Are you happy?"

"Well, I'm pretty happy—"

"Are you *proud* about not giving me a letter?"

Uh-oh. Against her hip, her chair twitches.

"Is that like your big accomplishment of the day? Not giving me something?"

"No, actually, I was—"

"Whatever." Christine walks off stage and gets her backpack. I reach into my pocket for Shakespeare but—ewwww—fingers grab mushy chocolate head and sink into soup ringed by foil! Abort mission! Chocolate filth!

"Wait, Christine—"

But she's already on her way out of the theater. She seems to walk slow, saying something to herself, maybe about Mr. Reyes, but more likely about me, I hope/fear, and then suddenly she's at the door and she scowls back once, as if thinking, Well, figured as much—his name's *Jeremy*. And then she's gone as if, you know, a giant dragon coiled its way up from the floor of the theater and decided to take her for its mate.

Fuck.

I should be pissed, right?

But, well . . . I'm weirdly relieved. It's like I knew this would happen all along. It's like I couldn't *handle* anything else; it's like this is the way the world works for me and what do you know, it worked again. Failure justifies all my worrying and planning and strategizing. I was right. I couldn't do it. It's almost as if I got away with something.

My posture is back to being no good, my un-slick peripheral vision has relaxed and I'm staring at the floor. I trudge to the bathroom to clean out my pocket.

seven

Middle Borough has changed. While I was reading *Midsummer Night's Dream*, industrious Student Union-ers were putting up announcements for the Halloween Dance, these cardstock pumpkins. They look like they should have a Hallmark logo on them somewhere, taped to the walls, holding each others' plump hands, dancing in circles. Pumpkins in love.

I go into the guys' bathroom. I stand in front of the sink and turn my right pocket inside out. It's not so bad; most of the Shakespeare stayed in the foil. I lick my fingertips as I remove it, soap up my hands and scrub the inner lining. It's peaceful here: a cracked-open window, the click-clack of the soap dispenser. . . . It's like that moment just after you leave the doctor's office, feeling all tingly and examined.

The door clangs. I try not to look—it's Rich, striding to the urinals and hitching up his pants like his penis is so huge, he has to take special precautionary measures getting it out. "What up, bitch?"

"Hey, Rich," I say, not moving. I've got to stop this, this deer-in-the-headlights freeze state that I go into whenever I'm confronted with girls or guys or even actual deer, or especially other guys' penises. . . .

"What'd you do, crap your pocket?" Rich asks over his shoulder as he pisses into the urinal. He's here after school for some manly sport.

"I don't talk to people who are pissing," I say. Only I don't say that.

Rich walks to the sink next to mine. He's probably still dripping. "Seriously, dude. What is that? You got chocolate in your pants?" He seems concerned.

"Yeah, well . . ."

"I'm not even gonna say the obvious thing about you being a fudge packer."

"Uh . . ." I don't really know what a fudge packer is, but when I think about it, it's pretty clear. Meanwhile, Rich laughs and calls me a bitch again. He leaves without washing his hands. I pull out my Humiliation Sheet and press it against the mirror with my wet wrist, scraping tally marks next to Laugh and Snotty Comment. It never ends with this school, and with Rich; for every one of him there are mini-hims like George or Ryu, and sometimes I think about renaming all of them, about standing inside the front door of Middle Borough on a stepladder and stamping their foreheads as they come in in the morning: Mouth Breather, Waste of Sperm, Ingrate, Troll, Skank, Retard, Pus Head, Junkie, Fetal Alcohol Casualty, Yellow Teeth, Stinky, Preggers, Soon to Be Featured on *World's Scariest Police Chases*, whack, whack, whack. I know them all so well.

Then I think about how among these people, these afterthoughts of all races and creeds, some are Cool and some aren't. How is that? It's something I've been wondering forever.

See, because being Cool is obviously the most important thing on earth. It's more important than getting a job, or having a girlfriend, or political power, or money, because all those things are predicated by Coolness. They happen because of it. They depend on it. I mean, Saddam Hussein was Cool; not that he's a good guy or anything, but he had to be pretty slick to get in power and keep it for so long. Alexander the Great was Cool. Henry Kissinger. Ben Franklin. Rick James. O.J. Bill Clinton. I'm not. I don't know why I'm not. I don't know how to change it. Maybe you're born with it. Maybe it skips a generation, because my parents are pretty popular people; they host little parties every few months. (I used to love them as a kid, hiding behind couches and stealing mini-sandwiches from the kitchen.) Maybe it all comes down to whether you were a bully or a chump in nursery school. Maybe that first confrontation is what does it, the first time you say "Screw it, this isn't worth fighting for," instead of "Screw you people, eat my fear."

Wherever Cool is, anyway, I missed it, and now I'm stuck observing these machinations of sex and status and dancing and parties and people sucking at each other under bleacher seating like some kind of freak, when I'm not the freak; Rich is the freak. Clearly. When I grow up, that had better be understood and I had better be compensated, or I'm going to shoot myself in the head.

eight

"How was school today?"

"Chocolate melted in my pants and I had a run-in with my short-statured tormentor." Only I don't say that. How can I explain this to Mom? Let's try the normal way: "Fine."

"That's good."

I'm sitting on the couch in front of the Bowflex machine in the living room. Mom bought Dad a Bowflex years ago in hopes he would exercise on it. She's bought him a lot of things—gym memberships, Slim-Fast, "Think Like a Thin Person" hypnosis tapes, liposuction consultations, Weight Watchers, Nautilus—but the Bowflex was the worst. Dad looked it over and decided the best place for it would be right between the couch and the TV; he now uses it exclusively as a rig to dry himself on in the morning after showering. Instead of toweling off he'll sit on the

Bowflex and flap towels under his crotch to CNBC; nobody bothers to move the machine during the day, so in the evenings it's still there, graced with the sweat of Dad's balls, as I eat microwave burritos with cheese and talk to Mom.

"Do you have lots of homework?"

"Nope."

"I'm *swamped* with work." Mom is in the dining room, which is basically the same as the living room, but with a curtain separating the two, so it's like I'm talking to the Wizard of Oz. "It's time to snip some nips, you know?"

That's a divorce term. Mom is a divorce lawyer. In fact, she's one of the most well-known divorce lawyers in central (non-Essex) New Jersey, with Dad, because of her bus ads. They run a firm together called Heere & Heere ("I should've kept my maiden name, Theyer," Mom jokes, but really her maiden name is Simonson) that advertises on buses in Trenton, New Brunswick, and Rahway. The ads say "Diamond's Don't HAVE to Be Forever" and show a gold ring being thrown into a hungry fire. I think it's great. I tell people I'm a child of divorce in an entirely different way from most kids.

"Yes, yes, a lot of Jersey couples are fed up right now. . . ." Mom continues to read documents. I can see her silhouette through the curtain; she's hunched over the dining room table behind stacks of envelopes.

"Mom, play rehearsal started today."

"What's your play called again?"

That's just what Mark asked, four hours ago. "*A Midsummer Night's Dream*."

"You know what play I love? *Cat on a Hot Tin Roof*. Are you going to do that one?"

"No, Mom. Is there any chance you could work with me on my lines sometime?"

"Ask your father. I'm busy."

"Dad's not home, Mom." I take the remote and turn the TV to my family's favorite show—whatever's on digital cable obscured by a big Bowflex shadow. Naturally, *Dismissed* fills my screen; it's always there in my lowest moments, so weird and dangerous and hypocritical that I'd like to shoot up my school just to blame it. I mean, what kind of show throws ménage-style blind dates at teenage boys? What are you telling them—all of a sudden, you're not Cool unless you're going out with *two* girls? You're entitled to *two* girls? Where's my *one* girl? And if you are a girl, are you better suited to competitive harem living than any sort of independent, self-sustaining existence, like Mom's doing right now behind her curtain? Are you bred for competition like a horse?

Naturally, MTV switches it around so girls go on a date with two guys or gay and lesbian people go out, but the result—cutthroat social contest, all day,

everyday; death to the ugly; death to the stam-
merers; death to the faces that got scarred in a
playground sometime—stays the same.

Still, one of the incredibly hot girls on *Dismissed*
is Asian. So I call up Michael Mell.

"Hey."

"Hey."

"You watching TV?" I hear his television click;
Michael sighs as he sees her. The contestants are on
a date in a junkyard. Michael is silent.

"So what's up," he finally says. "What happened
with Christine?"

"Oh, I, uh, started asking her about that letter, you
know, and she got pretty pissed off."

"Dumbass. Why'd you do that?"

Huh. I never considered that. Self-sabotage?

"I guess I just wanted to clear things up before pro-
ceeding."

"You talked to her, though, right?"

"Yeah."

"That's great, man."

"No, it's not. She's not talking to me anymore,
and I didn't give her the Shakespeare."

"Dude, I knew you weren't gonna give her the
Shakespeare. When I saw you at lunch, I knew *that*
wasn't gonna happen."

"Thanks," I say. "Anyway. What's up with you?"

"My brother is acting weird again. He just called.

He thinks the government is putting pills in people's brains."

"Ah, I see. Like that pill he got that got him through the SATs?"

"Yeah. But that one really happened."

"Sure."

"I'm telling you, man!" Michael says. "How could my brother get a 1530 on his SATs? How the hell is he going to Brown? He had this pill, I'm telling you."

"Sure. So listen." I have to refocus the conversation; Michael can go on and on. (On TV, the *Dismissed* threesome frolics in a hot-air balloon.) "Did you see the announcements for the Halloween Dance?"

"Nope. Do I care?"

"They went up late today."

"Yeah. And?"

"You think we should go?"

"Are you asking me out?"

"C'mon, Michael. Seriously. Why don't we go to a dance?"

"You should go. Christine will be there, right?"

Jeez, I didn't even think of that! Of course! "Yeah, she will!"

"So go. Good luck."

"What—am I supposed to go by myself?"

"Whoa! Whoa!" On TV, the *Dismissed* girls have taken to wrestling in some sort of oatmeal in their hot-air balloon. One of them has her top fuzzed out;

anytime anything gets fuzzed out on TV, Michael turns to his—

"De-Fuzzer time, baby!" My friend whoops— really, he can whoop; I picture him walking across his living room with the whoop-grin on his face to man the De-Fuzzer box. The De-Fuzzer is something that you can only attach to digital, flat-screen televisions and it costs $400 to get from some guys in New York. The quality of the unpixelation is really bootleg—it makes breasts look blocky and weird—but it works as advertised. Every time Michael turns it on, I'm understandably jealous.

"Daaaaaamn," he says. "Nice nipples. Dark."

"C'mon man, focus." I watch my boring, non-titty television. "I'm tired of this crap, looking at nipples or listening to you look at nipples. We have to get some real girls."

"No shit," Michael says. "But you know, it's not a good environment, evolutionarily, right now. Like, humanity is currently at its genetic peak. Did you know that?"

Michael's full of crap like this. I just wanted to talk about the dance.

"I read about it. Theoretically, we're all able to date whoever we want, whether they have bad eyesight or they're prone to disease or whatever. If you're a midget, you're still going to be able to find another midget and have good midget sex and breed, so we're not evolving anymore. No natural selection is taking place. In that sort of 'flat' climate, scientists think that instead of survival of the fittest, it's just survival of whoever's out there and uninhibited, you know. Confidence prevails. So we might be screwed."

"Thanks, man. I always knew I was screwed."

"No problem. Hey, I'm gonna watch the rest of this *Dismissed* by myself, cool?"

"Yeah, it's cool. Don't use Vaseline. See you tomorrow."

"See ya."

And I go into my room *(wop wop wop)* . . . to enter the Internet. I use it like most teenage boys do—exclusively for sex.

nine

Next morning I am determined to sort out who started the rumor about me and Christine and the letter.

Before that, though, I go to the bathroom to do an Appearance Check. I've been doing a lot of Appearance Checks lately. I've noticed that I'm kind of ugly. I mean, I have brown hair and brown eyes—good, right?—but under a critical light, which is how the world views you, I can see how I might resemble someone with palsy. My face is too long and the sockets that my eyes sit in are off-kilter size-wise, as if I were meant to have a larger eye on the left. My hair might be thick, but it's full of dandruff like a snowstorm. (Michael and I used to have dandruff battles, actually, ruffling our hair violently in a sunbeam to see who had more glittering scalp waste.) My lips are drawn back and ghoulish. My earlobes are huge. When I get enough money for plastic surgery, I'm going to start with—

"Goood morning," Dad says, ushering himself into the bathroom.

"Uh, hey," I say, breaking my stare with the mirror, turning the water on so it looks like I was washing my face. Dad is completely naked, as is usual before 10 A.M., except for his black socks. "Um, could I, um, get a little privacy in here?"

"Son, you're catching me midstream," Dad says.

"Yeah, I can *hear* that."

"Don't be embarrassed. Pretend we're in the army. No other heads available. Ten-hut."

"Dad, you were never *in* the army." I turn toward him, then regret it because his naked butt looks weird. It always looks like it's pressed up against a sheet of glass.

"How're my two boys in there?" Mom asks from outside in a singsong voice. "I've got to take a sho-wer!"

"Ho pippity pum pum!" Dad says, shaking his penis—

"Jesus, what is wrong with you people?"

"Jeremy?"

"Can you finish the second bathroom? *Please?*" I plant my hands on either side of the sink and close my eyes.

"Jeremy?" Mom asks, cracking the door open. Then, hissing at Dad: *"Put a towel on!"*

"It's not like he's a *girl*," Dad retorts. "We never

had a *girl*." I hear a soft ruffle as he grabs a towel and gets it around his wide body. Mom comes in and puts a hand on me. "What's wrong, Jeremy?"

"Nothing." I open my eyes and look at the mirror image of me and Mom, with her face slightly wrinkled before she gets the makeup in the creases, and Dad on the right, a naked fat face with a naked fat body, hands securing his towel like a happy Buddha. We look like an example of people who shouldn't breed and what their offspring would be.

"*Humuckuggg . . .*" I say. Then I stomp out of the bathroom, put on clothes, grab a fresh Humiliation Sheet and walk to school.

ten

I almost forgot about the walking to school. I live very close to Middle Borough—there's just one big field between it and my house and a gravel driveway that no one minds if I walk across and then seven trees and a pile of garbage and I'm there—so I walk.

It's weird to walk to school in Metuchen. Nobody walks to school. If you're a junior or a senior, you should absolutely have your own car and drive to school every day, and it had better be a shiny car with a multiple CD changer. If you're a sophomore and you're Cool then you should ride with one of the afore-mentioned juniors or seniors (it helps to have an older sibling—that's like an automatic Cool Person); if you're a dorky, weird, or impaired sophomore, you ride with your parents. If you're a freshman, you're for-given for riding with your parents, but it's your job to find peers who will give you rides when you hit soph-omore status. If you're poor, you ride the bus.

I walk, though, this morning like every morning, and once I get inside, Christine is at her usual spot at the front of math. I give her a look as I pass by; in fact I stare openly at her, apologetic, terrified, but she doesn't notice. I move to my seat.

Guess who Jenna is talking about today: "Then Elizabeth was like, 'But I don't know how to do it!' And the guy was like, 'All you do is take this resin and this chopstick—'"

"Be quiet," I say. "Everybody is sick of hearing about 'Elizabeth.'" Only I don't say that. Instead, I sit and look at Christine.

"There he goes again," Jenna says halfway through; I try not to notice.

"What?" Anne asks.

"The stalker, look at him." She nods her head at me the smallest bit.

"Oh, yeah." Anne turns around as if she's trying to pop the joints in her back. She looks at Jenna; Jenna gives a smiling look back; Anne looks slightly sad and pleading for me; Jenna responds with a withering look. I didn't realize girls could communicate like this, with their eyes, like evil monkeys.

"Don't say anything, he'll put it on one of his sheets," Jenna says.

Jenna knows about the Humiliation Sheets?

Fuck. The pit that forms in my stomach stretches down quickly to suck/tear at my bladder. If Jenna knows about the Humiliation Sheets, thirty other people do too. Cool People are like termites; for every one you see, there are thousands back at the hive with the same basic nervous system and worldview. I stare forward, as I usually do in times of crisis, not daring to note this particular offense on my sheet. Not yet.

eleven

"What's the deal?" Michael asks as I leave math. "You okay?" Michael's sitting cross-legged in the hall; I'm looking for a place to update my sheet.

"Yeah." I stoop down. I try to slap his hand, but miss.

"Redo," he smiles. We connect.

"All right. Take a seat."

"Why? I hate sitting on the floor."

"You should."

"Why?"

"Trust me."

I do.

"Anything new happen with Christine?" Michael prods.

"Nope. Today's been really crappy."

"Well it's about to get good." Michael absently picks at his headphone cord. "Take a look."

We are in the absolutely choicest position for spying girls' knees and calves in the hall. I figure that's what Michael plans to do, and then, across the way, a particularly fine parade of knees and calves emerges. They belong to Katrina, Stephanie, and Chloe—the Hottest Girls in School.

Michael is admirably calm as the three of them slink out of whatever class they were in (Human Sexuality, I think—seriously) in triangle formation with Katrina at the lead. I'm the one with the motor control problem, sitting like a tormented puppet, my wrist twitching and my neck grinding against itself as the legs pass by. My heart tightens and the whole lower half of my body aches in a sudden, silly way that reminds me of last night on the Internet.

"*Guh . . .*"

It's *unfair* that I should have to go to school with Katrina, Stephanie, and Chloe. They cover all the bases of things that you might possibly be attracted to if you think girls are attractive in the slightest bit. Katrina is blond, Stephanie is brunette, and Chloe is a redhead (dyed). Katrina wears bright, preppy stuff; Stephanie wears Goth things with collars; Chloe does raver clothes. All their outfits are tight and imaginative, as in: it's easy to imagine them not being there. The Hottest Girls in School came to Middle Borough together in my grade and have been inseparable since, a force to be reckoned with, discussed, analyzed, and penetrated by the upper echelon of Middle Borough men.

They do not react to Michael or myself in any way as they pass.

Then again, we are on the floor.

"You should go for one of them, man," Michael suggests.

"Shut up." Then: "You think I could?"

"Sure . . . You could do whatever you want. I mean, you're still going to that dance, right?"

I hadn't thought about the dance. I'd just been kind of talking about it the night before, in the abstract. Here in the light of day with real females present, the dance is more terrifying. I have not had good experiences with dances. I wasn't even good at those super-hippie modern dance "movement" classes I took in fifth grade. I couldn't be a spider right.

"I was kinda . . ."

Christine walks out of math. Maybe she was in there talking to Mr. Gretch, or one of her friends. She strides past me and I'm at eye level with her legs and calves and I think they might just be the most beautiful calves I've ever seen, better than the Hot Girls'. Then I think about how when computer imaging guys are making special effects for movies, one of the hardest things they have to do with CGI light is to get it to reflect off complex surfaces the right way, but if any of those CGI guys ever needed a model for how light should bounce off a girl's leg, pixel for pixel, this is it.

And the two forces that battle for real estate in my brain—fear and lust—they reach an agreement and I turn to Michael.

"Yeah, I'm going," I nod.

"Really?" He stands up.

"Yeah. You still not going?"

"That's the plan."

"Then could you give me a ride at least? After school or something? After play rehearsal, actually, down to Halloween Adventure sometime. So I can buy a costume."

"You're getting a costume and the whole deal? Who are you gonna bring to the dance?"

"I guess nobody. But"—I watch Christine fade—"I have to get there somehow."

twelve

I grab the seat next to Christine's for our second *Midsummer* read-through. (A girl named Jessica gets Mr. Reyes' Hot Pocket today, while we males construct a haphazard circle of chairs.) I don't know why; I'm just setting myself up for heartbreak, but I have fast reflexes and go with my instincts.

My arm shifts as we begin the reading. It inches so close to Christine's that static electricity pulls our armhairs together, my dark ones vs. her sunburned ones. If we both were to sweat, the beads would join up and form a little Bering Strait for microbes to swim across from her skin to mine. All I have to do now is pull a phrase out of the air, a phrase among all the trivia and trends and hot items in the world, that'll make her start talking to me like she did yesterday. A phrase like, *Wow, I heard this thing about Tupac's mom* or *I really like Picasso over Matisse*, but that might not be it. When I think about it, probably only one tenth of one tenth of one seventeenth of things are it.

"Hey, Christine, I heard this thing that human beings aren't evolving anymore."

"Wheh?" She turns with a mix of annoyance and bafflement. But what could I expect? It's a start.

"Yeah, seriously . . ." I glance over at Mr. Reyes; he's dozed off. "I heard about it on, uh, the Discovery Channel. We're totally evolutionarily stagnant."

Christine turns her pupils toward the sheet of paper on her lap. "'Through the forest have I gone But Athenian found I none, On whose eyes I might approve . . .'"

Right, I forgot. She has lines. When she finishes, she turns to me and says the most wonderful thing: "Actually, I heard that too."

"Really?" I almost forget to whisper.

"Of course not, Jeremy." Her lips curl beautifully. "Only you would know stuff like that. But it, uh, sounds interesting."

There's conspicuous silence around the circle. Christine pokes me (with her pen, not her actual flesh): "Your line."

"*Mrph* . . . 'Fair love, you faint with wand'ring in the wood. . . .'"

"Talk when rehearsal is over, okay?" Christine says.

I smile so wide that I check myself, because I know wide smiles make me look bad. Christine flicks her pen back and forth between her teeth.

I brush my arm against hers. Now that I've rebroken the ice, I knew I could rebreak the ice.

When the read-through is over, Christine and I chat. We put away chairs together. I give her the rap about people not evolving pretty much exactly as Michael gave it to me the night before.

". . . And so it's like we're evolutionarily flat."

"Wow, that's crazy." She's not betraying much. Her lips are pursed and that's a good word for it, because they look like a purse, an upside-down pink purse designed for a kangaroo rat or vole. "Don't you think that people are evolving to become *smarter*?"

"I think," I pontificate, "that women are naturally selecting males who are more successful and rich, but that has not much to do with whether they're smart." Heh-heh.

"Oh, no," Christine says, motioning with her hand for me to follow as she gathers her things. "Successful people are always smart."

"My dad's pretty successful. He's an idiot."

"That's not nice. What's he do?"

"Divorce lawyer. What's yours do?"

"Executive ride supervisor at Great Adventure."

"Oh, well, that must be a great adventure for his career!"

"Um . . . funny. He got fired, okay. He used to work for AOL—"

"No! No . . . I was just, you know, trying to think of something witty to say, like a pun or whatever."

"Uh-huh."

"Sorry." Pause. "I'm not a great conversationalist."

"But you were just having a conversation. We were."

"Yeah. Well. We're not. Now."

"This is true." Christine scrunches up her face. "You know what? I *hate* boys who are bad conversationalists." She shakes her head. "It's insurmountable."

Dur. Now she has her bag in her hands, but something's missing from it that perturbs her. She bends over a theater seat looking at the floor. I want to find the missing item desperately and be helpful. I think I've spotted it—a padded, white nub of material by her ankle. I reach down to pick it up; she leans back at the same time, sitting on my neck.

"Ow!"

"Hey!"

"Gimme that!" Christine streaks down, pushes me away and grabs the item off the floor.

"Sorry."

"*Hgggg,*" she chortles, putting the thing in her purse. Then she looks at me as if under a new light (an angry light, not a good light). "Jeremy, you shouldn't touch girls' *stuff*."

"I was just trying to help. . . ."

Christine walks away, so I walk with her; we pass through the doors of the theater together, separated only by the metal doorframe. "So I guess if your dad works at Great Adventure you don't have to worry about lines, right? I mean, lines at the rides. Not lines in the play. Heh-heh."

"Well . . ." Christine says. "First of all he's a ride supervisor, not a ride operator. Which means he works in an office, not on the ride."

"Okay."

"But yes, they do have this policy, if you're employee connected, where you walk up to the back of a ride and show them the special Great Adventure Friends and Family Card and then they give you this slip of paper that tells you the approximate ride wait time—"

"So?"

"So don't interrupt. So instead of waiting in line for forty-five minutes, you can do whatever you want for forty-five minutes and then come back and get right on."

"That's awesome! How do I get one of those cards? Do I have to marry you?"

Oh, shit. What did I just say?

"Uh . . ." Christine looks at me like I grew out of the base of a tree. "You could develop leprosy and lose half your face—that would work. Then you could get a handicapped pass."

We're halfway down the hall, heading toward the exit. I'm thinking of some witty final statement to make up for the marriage thing (did she say something about leprosy?) when I spot a figure at the doors: Jake Dillinger. He looks all Czechoslovakian-model-banging and student-governmental. He cups his mouth.

"—Jeremy—" is all I can make from down the hall; he must be saying hi to me. Jake parcels out whole tenths of a second when he sees me. Then he looks at Christine. He doesn't need to say anything to her.

"Gotta go!" Christine says. "Talk tomorrow!" And she skips down the hall to meet Jake, like Puck would skip, as if he had worked some magic on her yesterday that went completely over my head. I swivel around quickly so I don't have to see them hug or tongue or dry hump, greet each other in whatever way they've picked. Then I walk out the back door of Middle Borough.

thirteen

Michael's there, in the school parking lot. He managed to borrow the car from his parents and have it waiting for me the day I asked for it. I hug him.

"What's up?" Michael's got a handball—he was probably playing for money while I was in rehearsal. He tosses it lazily against the mural in the back of school.

"Same crap is up," I say. "Christine, who I thought was at least available, is with Jake *Dillinger*."

"That's messed," Michael shakes his head. "But you gotta give other men credit, y'know?"

"No. I don't know."

Michael tosses the handball at me. I try to catch but it bounces off my fingers and chin. "C'mon," he says. "Throw the ball at the wall. See the wall?"

"Shut up." I rear back and throw pretty hard; the ball rebounds and Michael lunges to hit it, seemingly with his wrist—there's a *pop*. I look over, but he's grinning, not hurt, as the ball comes hurtling back toward me. It hits my skull and careens off under some school administrator's car. Michael and I laugh.

"C'mon," he says, "We got like twenty minutes if you really want to go to Halloween Adventure."

"Okay." We head to Michael's car.

I've never been entirely sure what Michael's driving status is; he probably has a learner's permit that doesn't allow him to drive by himself, but since you can't violate any laws in a huge brown Buick going 25 mph, we stay out of trouble. I slip inside—it smells like burned peanut butter and ham.

Michael puts some God-awful emo tape on. I look out the window as we roll away from school.

"Oh, I forgot, you hate this, right?" Michael asks, pointing at the music. "I can play *Pinkerton*."

"It's okay," I say. Michael can put on whatever music he wants (except maybe *Pinkerton*) because I love driving. I've always loved it. I never understood how little kids can ask "Are we there yet?" or want to pee all the time—since I was two, when the family had the Volvo, I've been content to hang my head out the window and just watch the scenery. I used to like seeing houses and hills that I hadn't seen before, but this is Jersey—that got old quick. So now I do this thing: I look at houses and speculate about the *people* inside. Are they old? Are they pretty? Are they girls that like me?

"So tell me," Michael breaches. "How come you want Christine so bad?"

I turn to him. "Um, I dig her."

"How come?"

"She's hot." I catch myself: "She's smart too."

"And you don't want to just hook up with her? You want to *date* her and stuff?"

"Yeah!"

"Huh. Do you like your shirts?"

I look down at what I'm wearing: a *Star Wars Episode I* T-shirt. "They're okay, I guess."

"Well, if you like your shirts, you might not want to date any girls. Girls are like the arch nemeses of shirts," Michael says.

"Really."

"Oh yeah. Shirts are their trophies. The last girl my brother went out with, she ended up with like three of his shirts. He used to come home wearing a jacket and no shirt. Don't go dating girls unless you're willing to lose your shirts. You might just want to do whatever and the girls will show up eventually and *not* take your shirts."

"Hey, Michael." I almost forgot. "What's up with that thing your brother had? The pill that made him smart? How did that work again?"

"I thought you didn't believe in that."

"Well it's tough to imagine he got a 1530 on his SATs."

"Heh. Yeah. Well, I told you."

"He had electronic assistance or something? I mean, I heard about these guys at Columbia—"

"No, man," Michael says, gripping the wheel. "This is a totally different thing. I think it's called a 'script.'"

I look at him carefully.

"Like it scripts in your mind, so it's a 'script,' this computer that comes in a pill, y'know? Experimental shit the government is doing."

"Okay. And he really had one?"

"Yeah." Michael pulls up to Halloween Adventure. "Go quick, they're almost closed."

I go into the store thinking about the script, but forget it pretty quickly because I have to beg the attendant for a little extra time to track down and pay for a *Scary Movie* mask. It's so dumb; it almost dares me to buy it. I figure with it on, no one'll be able to recognize me and all I'll have to do is wear black pants and a black shirt, and if I get Christine alone and we have that amazing high-school romantic movie moment, with drinking and young lust and strawberry-flavored lip gloss, I can rip the mask off and she can see me for who I really am and we'll start having sex against a tree maybe and—

"Jesus," Michael says as I walk out of the store with the mask on. "You're the one that needs the pill, man; that is *stupid*."

fourteen

The next week, in play rehearsal, I fall into a pattern with Christine. (What does it take for a behavior to become a pattern? One repetition, right?) I come in, grab the seat next to her and bumblingly mention a quasi-fact about music or current events or evolution, often stolen from Michael. She humors me (or maybe not, sometimes she seems to smile humor-free) with comments of her own, and we build that, falteringly, into a conversation that ends five minutes after play rehearsal and then she runs off to meet Jake. Only I don't know what to make of her and Jake. They never talk to each other during rehearsal; he sits across the circle from her and eyes her only occasionally. Is it possible they're just friends?

That's one thing I hate about, uh, the world. I hate touchy-feely friend relationships between guys and girls. I hate them when I'm in them, of course, but I'm not in them too often so mostly I just hate them from outside. They're confusing and complicating: if you're a girl and you're touching a guy's leg, I'm going to assume you're going out. End of story. If you are actually platonic friends, don't put your heads in each other's laps and don't kiss each other on the lips. Right now we are living in one of the first periods of human existence where young men and women can actually *be* friends without pending marriage or negotiations over which family has which tracts of land. So don't mess with it.

Christine, despite the fact that she is a prime offender of this nature, has a system of stages that she uses to keep things straight. She explains them to me after play rehearsal Friday. (One week to the dance.)

"Everybody needs to be on my system," she says, standing by her seat in the audience rows, rifling through her bag as I keep my eyes glued to her. "It's like, the only way." She swishes a grin at me. "There are four stages of a relationship, see?"

"Uh-huh." My hands are clasped over my crotch like a soccer player's.

"Okay, first, there's Hooking Up."

Boy. I hate that one. "Hooking Up" is what *I'm* supposed to be doing, one way or another. The magic phrase for two types of young Americans: unimpeded teenage sex for the Cool ones, kissing for me and Michael and the rest of the unearmarked sludge. Yay!

"—or anything," Christine says.

"Wait, no! I missed that," I apologize. "Could you say it again?"

"Well, I just went over Hooking Up," she says. "Hooking Up is the first stage. That means you have someone who you've, y'know, *hooked up* with and maybe done other things with, but there are no commitment strings anywhere. You don't call this person up. You don't sit with him anywhere. You just did what you did and that's it."

"What does it mean, like, sex-wise?"

"Depending on whether or not you're a slut," Christine says, "Hooking Up means having sex. Which I totally understand, for some people. But we're talking about my system. Skanky girls work on their own system. You want to sit?"

"Sure."

She continues with her elbow on the armrest between us. The armrest is dirty and her elbow is not.

"Stage two is Dating. Dating occurs after Hooking Up when you and the guy actually show up at public places together and give people the impression that you're more than friends by kissing and touching." That sounds like where Christine is with Jake, but I don't want to ask. Jake is across the room talking to one of his football underlings. "Dating has no commitment either. Like, you can see other people and you don't have to tell the person you're dating, see?"

"Uh-huh."

"Stage three is Going Out. Going Out is like Dating with a little more commitment. At this point, you know, sex might be a consideration, so if you *are* having sex with the person you're going out with, then you can't have sex with anybody else." I like hearing Christine talk about sex. It could be sex with those toads that have other toads spring out of their backs, whatever. "But if you accidentally *do* have sex with someone else, then you are legally obligated—or rather, obligated by my system, which is just as good as legally obligated—to tell the person you are going out with. Then collectively you can make a decision on whether you want to continue the relationship, given your transgression. You know 'transgression,' right?"

"Yeah." Vocab pays off! "So how is Going Out different from Dating?"

"Um . . . let's see. . . . in Dating, you hold hands, maybe. In Going Out, you put your arm around me or whatever."

Huh. "What's the last stage?"

"The best one!" Christine throws up her arms. "Boyfriend–Girlfriend. That's like, you're totally devoted to each other, no questions asked, you absolutely cannot have any kind of contact with anybody else by penalty of whatever I decide."

"What if it's you who cheats and the guy who has to decide the penalty?"

"I don't cheat."

"Oh. That's good."

"I think so." Christine smiles.

"You forgot Stage Five, after Boyfriend–Girlfriend." I tilt my head back, feeling a witticism coming on.

"What's that?"

"*Ex* Boyfriend–Girlfriend!"

"Shut up!" Christine hits me in the arm with her small balled fist. Jake shows up, shadows us both.

"Hey, Jeremy," he says, turning on his cyborg kindness. Then he looks at Christine intensely. "Christine."

"Yeah?" She twists around. Her body is poised to punch me again, but all I can see of her face is a twisted neck.

"You want to get outta here?"

"Sure!" she chirps. "Bye, Jeremy!" she turns back and kisses me on the cheek. Our first kiss. She gets up and steps into Jake, who slips an arm around her jeans-encased butt as they walk off.

Going Out. At least now I know which stage I'm up against. I'm getting prepped. I think I might have a shot.

fifteen

The Halloween Dance doesn't happen at Middle Borough High School. It happens at a bar/dance hall near the poor section of Metuchen called the Elks Club Lodge, a place for old men to drink and play pool.

I can't get to the Club by myself. It's almost in Edison, the next town over from Metuchen, and Michael really isn't going because he's listening to the new Weezer album. There is the option of getting my parents to drive me to the dance, but I decide against that particular form of self-hatred. I dial up a car service and approach Mom as she works in the dining room, to tell her the deal.

"Hey, Mom?"

"Yes, Jeremy." She doesn't look up from her work.

"There's actually a, ah, Halloween Dance tonight as part of school, so I'm going."

"Really?" Mom asks, looking up. And just as her

really is ending, Dad slips through the curtain into the dining room, shirtless. He's eating a giant hot dog in a too-small bun. "Really?" he says.

"Yeah!" I look back and forth between Dad and Mom. I had expected challenges.

"That's wonderful!" Mom gets up and hugs me. "Who are you going with?"

"Yeah, what's up?" Dad asks. "Does she have, you know . . ." Dad pantomimes breasts with his hands and hot dog.

"Stop it!" Mom snaps. "That is *not* appropriate."

"You'd be surprised, son," Dad says. "So many divorces that I handle stem from breasts. They're incredibly important. Make sure that the girl—"

"There isn't a girl," I declare.

Silence from Mom.

"Hmm," Dad chews. "Are you gay?"

"Stop it!" Mom shrieks, scrambling toward Dad. He skitters out. "Your father," she says, returning to her seat at the stacks of paper. "Sometimes I really don't know. So, in any case—"

"I'm not gay. Don't worry."

"I'm not," Mom smiles. "It would be fine if you were, really. We're good parents. But you're going to a dance?"

"Yeah."

"That's great. Do you need money?"

"Sure." I had no idea they'd give me money

for this. I suppose I should be more social more often.

"Here," Mom presses bills into my hands that I'll count later. "Go to the dance—do you need a ride? Oh wait, I'm sure you wouldn't want one from us. Take a car service!"

"Yeah, I already called one."

"Well that's great! Remember, don't ever touch my car, Jeremy. But have fun at the dance! You'll do fine."

"Yeah, for sure!" Dad says from the living room, eating his hot dog on the Bowflex. "Dance with girls!"

"Thanks, Dad." I walk out to the porch and wait for the car service. When it comes, I stroll down the lawn dressed entirely in black, mask over the top of my head, not on. I get in the car and try to negotiate the wannabe-strawberry air-freshener smell.

"Where you goin'?" the driver asks.

"Elks Club Lodge, Lefferts Road by the Friendly's."

"T'anks." We slide down my street, take a turn past school and the field, which somehow has two fireflies in it, spinning in a lazy DNA spiral, this late in the year. I try my mask on.

"Oooh, tha's cool," the driver says.

"Yeah?"

"Yeah. You look like a l'il hooligan."

Hooligan? Hooligan doesn't sound particularly dangerous or interesting. We ride in silence the rest of the way. I plan the night's events: if Christine is there with Jake, I'll pay a girl some of this money Mom gave me to distract Jake while I talk with Christine about how I feel about her (good plan). Then I'll take off my mask and she'll see who I am and she'll be like—

"We here," the driver says. I pay him and step out.

The Elks Club Lodge has a snaking line in front of it nine trees long, comprised of kids dressed as pro wrestlers, kids dressed as members of Slipknot, kids dressed as Fidel Castro and Bill Clinton with Phillies in their masked mouths, kids dressed as giant condoms and Viagra pills. The line surprises me. I step to the back with my mask down.

"What's this for?" I ask the guy in front of me.

"Tickets, yo," he says over his shoulder, making a lip-smacking noise. He's dressed as some sort of small tree. "You need tickets for the dance."

Oh crap, it's Rich. His whole face is green, so I couldn't tell at first. I'd better be quiet so he doesn't figure out who I am and torment me. I keep the mask on and it gets atrocious and spitty inside, but I think the anonymity is worth it. The line shuffles toward the door and I finally get in after giving money to a guy who looks like a walrus.

The Elks Club Lodge is perfect for the Halloween Dance; it looks like a Scooby-Doo mansion inside. Fake cobwebs hang out with real ones. Streams of orange tissue paper buddy up with actual mold on the ceiling. In the music room, a small platform has been constructed on which a DJ dressed as a wizard distributes choice R&B.

"Ngukkk!" someone yells as they fly by me swinging a sword. Samurai costume. The samurai stashes his weapon by a pipe and starts dancing as I make for the punch.

"Welcome to the dance," Ms. Rayburn says, ladling out a cup that has a piece of pineapple floating in it. "Nice mask, hope we get to see who you are later, huh?" Ms. Rayburn smiles; she's dressed as a librarian/secretary and is exceedingly hot. Then I take a look at the dance floor and get a whole new definition of exceedingly hot.

Katrina, Stephanie, and Chloe are here! That accounts for the long line and characters like Rich— where the Hot Girls go, people follow. They're in the center of the room, gyrating, a mesmerizing Amazon bundle. Katrina is dressed as a French maid with the little skirt and feather duster, only her outfit is blue instead of black; Stephanie is a bondage Goth, which isn't too far away from her normal wear, just with a bigger collar; Chloe has on small orange cat ears and a tail like an impish tiger-girl. It's Chloe I stare at most hungrily (sometime tonight I've got to find pics on the Internet of girls with tails) as I slide up to a row of guys by the wooden Elks Club walls. They're standing, doing exactly what I'm doing—scoping the Hot Girls, bopping their heads in a range of millimeters to the R&B.

I stand at the end of the line, next to a kid named Eric who was probably too stoned to bother with a costume; he just sports his huge eyebrow, which I know is natural. Next to Eric is Rodney, dressed as a postal worker with a chainsaw, and toward the end of the line is Mark Jackson from math—he's the only one who'd come as Game Boy SP.

I pick my foot up and press the sole of my shoe flat against the wall. I should be as comfortable with my wallflower status as these guys are—the way they position their shoulders and backs and hips is almost a dance of its own. I'm not there more than two minutes when Rich, in that strange tree costume, approaches.

"Hey," he actually says to me.

I clench up inside my mask. What does he want? He stands with his back to the wall and keeps quiet, alternating sips of punch with sips from an old-timey hip flask stashed in one of his many pockets.

"Want some?" he asks, shrugging his flask in my direction. What the hell is this? Does he not know who I am? I turn toward him in my mask and he smirks at it. I take his flask, slip it under my chin and suck down a big swig. Then another.

"No way," Rich says. "You're like the alky ghost, dude." I don't know what's in the flask, but it burns and cracks my throat as it goes down. "Bleccch, jeez," I gargle through my mouth hole.

"Scotch," Rich says.

"Yecch."

Rich looks down. "So it's Jeremy Heere under that mask, right?"

"Yeah." Uh-oh.

"Is it true what I heard, Jeremy? You keep sheets of paper and write down all the shit that happens to you, like a list?"

"Yeah," I gulp. The Humiliation Sheets are out.

"Well," Rich says. "I'm sure I'm on them a lot." He looks at me with open eyes, with some kind of understanding and humanity. Then he turns back to the dance floor. "So which one would you get with?" He gestures to the Hot Girls.

"Uh, Chloe," I confide.

"Bad choice, man. You gotta go with Katrina. I mean, she looks just like Barbie. I've wanted to fuck Barbie since I was *born*—"

In the midst of this ridiculousness (Rich is drunk, I figure), I see Christine. Actually I see her head, shrouded by a Rapunzel-style red-and-gold princess hat, bobbing to the left of the Hot Girl entanglement. As she moves into full view, I see that she's dressed like a Persian prostitute/angel, with a gold halter top, glitter all over her belly, and puffy pink pants like Jasmine in *Aladdin* (only Jasmine's might not have been pink). The thing is, she has giant, golden wings affixed to her shoulders; they wreak havoc on her dancing. It's such a mess, but cute somehow; I picture her dressing up in her room and thinking how it would impress Jake.

". . . Now, the problem with Chloe is that she has no idea about how panties are supposed to be worn—" Rich continues, but I'm actually ignoring him, because Jake Dillinger is on the floor with Christine. Damn. He's not wearing any costume, just a tuxedo. He's dancing the absolutely best way a white guy can, planting his feet and leaning back and letting the girl rub herself all over him. And Christine rubs herself expertly. She rubs herself on him like she was trying to get barnacles off the backs of her upper thighs. The wings make Jake flinch.

"—And she had this threesome with the girls from *Friends*, but it wasn't even a threesome, it was a *four-some*—" Rich explains.

Now Christine bends over, putting her butt right on the place where Jake's no-doubt-impressive penis hoists on a likely nightly basis—

"Hey, you wanna talk to that girl?" Rich asks.

"Uh, what?"

"C'mon, Jeremy, you're not even paying attention to me. You want that girl?"

"Well . . ." Why lie? Just say it. "Sure. Yeah. Of course I do."

"You realize I could walk right up to her right now and get her to fuck me?" Rich smiles. "Anytime."

"Um, actually I wouldn't doubt that. You seem to do okay with the girls in our school."

"'Okay?'" Rich looks offended by my very presence, which is a look I'm used to. "Okay my ass. Watch this."

Rich walks across the dance floor and starts talking to another girl named Samartha, a pretty hot one with punch in her hand standing by the opposite wall. After chatting for about three minutes, he lounges on a nearby Ping-Pong table. Samartha comes over and kisses him. I watch intensely; Rich whispers in her ear and she begins to lick and suck his belly button with one high-heeled foot bent behind her so the heel touches her butt cheek, which is blue, with stars. (She's Wonder Woman.) After a minute of that, Rich gets up, kisses her, and walks back to me.

"You see?" he says. "That's real pimpin'."

"Yeah."

"Real pimpin', but not *natural* pimpin'. I had help."

"Uh . . ."

"I got a squip, man."

"You're quick?"

"Not quick. A 'squip.'"

"Ohhh . . . " Flashes flash in my head. "The 'script.'"

"No, 'squip.'"

"I think I've heard of it—"

"Not script. Squip."

"Wait. What?"

"The squip," Rich says, and the way he says it I kind of know that something is starting, something is happening, and I'm glad because anything would be better than me in this mask not dancing with any girls, watching Rich get his belly button licked. "And *you* need a squip, man. You need it more than, like, anyone I know. You're almost hopeless. That's why I'm telling you. You have to get squipped."

"Yeah, well, I think I heard about it from my friend," I say carefully, not wanting to step on this and make it go away. "What is it?"

"It's a cool pill," he says. "From Japan."

"Like, it makes you smarter I heard? I thought—"

"You didn't think nothing. Look."

Rich opens his fist and for the first time I realize what he's dressed as—a giant weed leaf. Isn't that great? I look down and there's a gray oblong pill nestled like a wart in the light creases of his palm. It looks like the acidophilus supplements Mom used to give me as a kid.

"What's it do?" I ask. "Is it drugs?"

"Heh, no, it's not drugs," Rich says, closing his fist. "It's better than drugs. It's a supercomputer, a quantum nanotechnology CPU that fits in a pill."

"Really?"

"Yeah. Like, they are way ahead of us with this stuff in Japan but it's going to hit the American markets soon." As Rich talks, rap blares, something heavily dependent on barking. Rich almost sounds like he's doing a sales pitch: "You take it, you know, *ingest* it, and the quantum computer, which is inside the pill, travels through your bloodstream and up into you brain. Then it sits in your brain and assists you."

"How?"

"It's preprogrammed. Once it gets up there, it tells you how to be cool all the time. It interacts with your brain as if it were a voice talking to you."

"Are you for real?"

"See, if you were squipped, you wouldn't say that," Rich smirks. "You wouldn't use outdated terminology and clunky phrasing like that."

"Ah . . ."

"And I gotta say, I'm personally sorry for treating you like a piece of garbage all the time." Rich looks humble and reverent. "I only do it because my squip tells me to. It advised me that I'd have to be a dick to you for social reasons, but recently it started saying that you were a decent guy actually who might want a squip of your own."

"Uh . . . apology accepted," I gurgle. The DJ has put on a slow song and Christine and Jake are kissing (hooking up) on the dance floor, but I don't care. I'm rapt. "So this is like, a real thing. You aren't BS-ing me."

"Once again, you wouldn't say 'BS-ing' if you had one," Rich says. "And yeah, it's real. This one I have here was going to be bought by Ryu tonight, but he never showed."

"How long does it last?"

"I think it's permanent. I've had mine four months. Now, do you even remember me four months ago?"

"It was summer."

"Right, but what about last year?"

"Last year I didn't see you much."

"Nobody saw me, because I was busy jerking off on the Internet, I was such a loser," Rich explains. "My squip fixed that, okay?"

"Huh."

"Squips are awesome. Mine is actually off right now, because I'm talking to you and not some hottie, but when it's on, it's great. . . . First thing it did was instruct me how to get consistent ass. It was very specific. Then it told me to start doing sports to cut my muscles a little and make me appeal to girls more. Then it told me who to piss off and who to be friends with, of which you were a minor part. Then it got me with all three of the Hot Girls to solidify my social standing. It hasn't let up."

"Damn. You've been with all *three* of them?" It might be the scotch or a contact high from Eric's eyebrow, but I don't think Rich is lying. I think there might have been a reason for me to be here tonight, besides Christine, who's the real reason for everything. Somebody has made a pill for idiots like me and now all I need is—

"Where do I get one?" I ask about ten times more eagerly than I would have liked. (Will my squip fix that?)

"Why do you think I'm telling you all this?" Rich asks. "You get one through *me*. I got a supplier who exports leather down at the bowling alley in New Brunswick—"

"The big bowling alley?"

"Yeah. Now this guy's from Ghana, so he's not around all the time, but I can reserve a pill for you. I would need two hundred now, four hundred when it comes in."

"Um . . ." My brain struggles with $200 + 400 = ?$ "I don't have six hundred bucks."

"You're screwed, then!" Rich says gleefully. Then he puts a hand on my shoulder. "No, seriously, not really; maybe we could work something out. Talk to me or Keith back at school."

"Keith the football player? With the tattoos?"

"God, you really need one, Jeremy. Yes, with the tattoos. He knows."

"Okay. Cool," I say.

"Most definitely. I mean we could all use a little thing in our brains getting us laid by high school girls all the time, right?"

"I could."

"Yeah. So keep in touch. And in the meantime, you want me to talk to, ah, the Queen of Wherever over there?" Rich points at Christine. "Maybe I could get her to fuck *you*." Christine has her arms around Jake's neck, Rapunzel hat leaning off to the side, wings akimbo.

"No," I say lightly.

"A'ight." Rich shrugs and leaves. "Remember," he says, pointing to his head as he goes back to Samartha. "Uh!" And he makes a little noise of triumph.

Not knowing what else to do, forgetting my original plan (did I have one?), I walk out of the dance. The doorman is reading a pornographic Mexican comic book with a woman dressed as an armadillo having sex with a coat rack. He jerks up, surprised to see me go so early. I reach the road and turn left; I've got enough money for a car home, but I have to walk tonight, three miles along route 27, taking it all in. People must think I'm the world's oldest, loneliest, most confused trick-or-treater, but cops and motorists leave me alone, and when I get back to my house at 2:17 A.M., Mom is worried, but Dad is happy. He figures I got with some girl at the dance—that must've been what took me so long. I don't want to disappoint him, so I go into my room all smiling and lie down with my head buzzing around the word *squip*.

sixteen

The next morning (well, technically, I wake up at noon), I go to Google. Type in *squip*: 361 results. The first one takes me to a dinky Web fighting game where you're a small alien who can battle an opposing alien with your gigantic nose. I play twice, learn how to win every time, and click back. The second link is more on-target, from Yahoo News.

Sony Hints at Next Generation of Wearable Computers

Just as the Segway Human Transport system was introduced to the world as clandestine, heavily-funded "IT" technology, digital designers and futurists are now buzzing about "SQUIP" as the next great leap forward in human lifestyle enhancement. SQUIP is being developed by **Sony** (SNE).

"It's a simple device that will redefine how computers operate within our society," says Harvey Dinglesnort about SQUIP, which Sony refuses to comment on directly. Mr. Dinglesnort reviews high-end devices for a variety of publications including **The Sharper Image** (SHRP). "They're keeping close tabs on it because it really will be a sensation when it is released."

What is known about SQUIP is that it involves micro-computers that can be implanted—or ingested—into the human body. Devices like the VeriChip, from **Applied Digital Systems** (ADSXE), already provide this functionality, but VeriChip implantation is a surgical procedure (albeit an outpatient one) involving a needle large enough to dose an elephant. SQUIP is said to be much smaller and easier to "install" due to the fact that it does not employ conventional microchip structure.

"Sony is going consumer with quantum computing," Mr. Dinglesnort explains. "Scientists have been researching for years the prospect of building a computer based not on the binary system, where a piece of information is either a one or a zero, but on a 'qubit' system, where a piece of information can be a one, a zero, or a sort of in-between state that collapses into a one or zero when it is observed closely."

The quantum computer is of interest to researchers because of its staggering data-processing capabilities, exponentially surpassing those of current CPUs. It has been discussed for projects ranging from large-scale materials fabrication to time travel. But Sony seems to have simpler plans.

"What they have said is, 'Let's not worry about all the great things quantum computers can do. Let's just make a simple one and take advantage of the fact that it can be tiny, and try to manufacture a sort of ingestible **Palm Pilot**,'" Mr. Dinglesnort says. Consumer models are a long way off. But the prospect of SQUIP has futurists drooling and investors lining up and . . .

I hit CONTROL N on my computer, open a new window for porn, and jerk off as I read. It seems that every site has the same information about the squip (or SQUIP; capitalization doesn't matter): Sony is working on it, but nobody knows what it is. It involves tiny computers that you eat. It's not out and won't be for a while. That means bootleggers must have escaped Japan with it and brought it to central New Jersey, where it took root among scotch-drinking high school kids. That isn't so far-fetched.

Unfortunately, there's nowhere I can buy a squip. There are no sites that offer it with a little shopping cart next to it. There's no way to determine if $600 is a fair price for one. And there's no guarantee that it's safe and won't take over my brain and turn me into a . . . I dunno, something worse than I am now, there has to be something, a mongoloid or—

"Jeremy!" Mom calls from the kitchen. "Phone!"

I pick up, knowing it's Michael before my spittle hits the receiver. "Hi."

"Are you feeling okay?!" Mom calls again. "It's *one o'clock*!"

"I'm on the *phone*!"

"Can you talk?" Michael asks, testing.

"Yeah."

"How was it?"

"Dance was really weird," I say. "Christine, whatever, uh . . . do you remember—" I stop.

"Remember what?"

"No. Forget it." I think about things for a second. I don't want to give Michael crucial information that'll help him get his hands on a squip. He does all right with the Asian girls at Middle Borough; he ends up talking to ones you never noticed—but are actually pretty hot—and he dated one last year for more than a week. He doesn't need a mechanical advantage the way I do. Let him find out on his own.

"Um . . . okay. So what are you doing?"

I'm masturbating still, watching a video, but it's not like I'm masturbating *to* Michael. I'm multitasking masturbating. "Checking the Web for some stuff," I say.

"Cool. What are you up to the rest of today?"

"I want to go down to the bowling alley in New Brunswick, ask around for some people, you know?"

"'Some people?'"

"Yeah," I chuckle. "I've got this project in mind. You wanna go?"

"No."

"What are you doing today?"

"Chilling out, listening to music."

"Michael, you do that every weekend."

"Yeah . . ." He stews a while. I click the mouse.

"How about you do something different? Come with me down to the bowling alley. It'll be fun."

"Okay, see—" Michael has a lot of protests and it takes a while to convince him, but I do. Once we hang up, I finish with the porn and my garbage can and head out of the house and swing into Michael's waiting car. I guess I have more influence on my friend than I thought. I look at his profile as we drive off: he should've been at the dance. Somebody would have dug him. If he had a squip, I'm sure, it wouldn't just let him sit and listen to Weezer all the time. He might need one after I get mine.

seventeen

It's 4 P.M. by the time we get to the B. Bowl-Town bowling alley; the place is clogged with matted, shrill children sending balls down lanes whose gutters have been filled with blue balloons to prevent failure. Even with these giant bowling prophylactics, kids mess up, aiming for the space between pins 7 and 10 and the unprotected back gutter or ricocheting their balls slowly off the barriers until they kiss the pins for zero points. The mothers, each of whom seems to be helming her own six-year-old birthday party, must then shelter and comfort the youngsters and explain that bowling is just a game and it doesn't matter if Timmy Banana has thirty-seven points when you have twelve.

I stand by the candy machine, one foot pressed against the bowling-alley off-white wall. I like this stance; now that I found it at the dance I'm sticking with it. I keep a lookout for Rich or, even better, the importer from Ghana who had the squips in the first place. Michael is on the other side of the vending machine.

A textbook youth approaches us. The silver chain connecting his nose and ear shadows a chain of itchy-looking lumps in the same place.

"Heard of the 'squip'?" I whisper.

The kid takes a quick look at me, makes a rodent face of confusion, and gets a bag of Cheez-Its.

"Jeremy, why are we here?" Michael leans over. "Who are you waiting for?"

"I'm not waiting for anybody. I'm *looking* for somebody."

"Well, go ask at the bar." Michael points to the rectangular wood countertop with glasses hanging from the ceiling that serves as a bar in this place. "You're supposed to ask for people and investigate stuff at the *bar*. Haven't you seen movies?"

"Yeah, okay. Thanks." I walk over there. There's a woman with red hair and nested wrinkles behind the counter.

"You gotta be kidding," she huffs.

"Don't worry," I say, putting my elbow down on the wood and covering my mouth. "I'm not trying to 'drink'. I'm looking for somebody."

"Get your arm off my bar. You've still gotta be kidding." She takes a glass down from the ceiling, fills it with ice and pops a cube in her mouth. "Who are you looking for?"

"This guy who, ah, imports leather from Ghana," I explain. "He'd probably be a black guy. . . ."

"Would he?" asks the only other character at the bar, an Asian man opposite me and Ms. Bartender.

"Right." I stare at this man, this new entry in my database.

"Why don't you come over here?" he sneers. "I know you kids. You're all after the same thing. You think you're the first one to go snooping for them?"

Whoa. I sidle over to the guy. He isn't too old. Badly dressed in a T-shirt, biking shorts, and an Eagles hat. White spiky hairs on his chin and little cuts on his cheek. Dull black eyes, all pupil.

"Hi," I reach my hand out. "I'm Jeremy Heere."

"You in it to win it?" he shoots back, holding his drink. "You in this for real? You want to change your life with this thing?"

"Yes," I nod.

"Well you're late," he says. "They're all gone. Latest shipment got dispersed, and I'm not sure about the authenticity of the next batch. Things are getting tight. Pretty soon you might not be able to get one anywhere. Until a few years, of course, when they're mass released."

"Uh-huh. I can't wait a few years." In a few years, I'll be old and then I won't need to be Cool. Just rich. I think it's harder to be Cool than rich. I move to stand a little bit behind the guy's barstool so I won't get Ms. Bartender in trouble.

"Who told you about me?" he asks out the side of his mouth. "Keith? Rich?"

"Rich."

"Idiot. Shouldn't be sending kids over to me. Tell him I'm gonna cut him off if he forwards any more kids to me. No, wait, don't say I'm gonna 'cut him off'; say I'm gonna 'cut him.'" The man chuckles. "That's good, right?"

"How do I get my squip?" I whine. "I was going to buy it from Rich, or from you!"

"Do two things," the man says. "Go to my cousin's store in the Menlo Park Mall. He works at Payless Shoes in there. Well, actually there are three Payless Shoes, but he's at the one opposite Sam Goody. Well, actually there are two Sam Goodys, but anyway, his name's Rack, like a spice rack. Talk to him about where the last coupla pills went. And try eBay."

"eBay?"

"Yeah, you have a computer, right? You'd be amazed."

"One more question," I look at my shoes. "Once I track a squip down, is it really going to cost six hundred bucks?"

"Maybe five. But c'mere," the man swivels toward me in his stool. "Look." He opens his wallet and an accordion of photographs, like the one my grandmother used to have, spills forth. They're photographs of him inside large, elaborate casinos—I guess it's Las Vegas, but you never know; it could be Foxwoods or some offshore place or something.

"Check 'em," he instructs. "Take a good look."

Each photo is a shot of this ragged man winning *large* amounts of money—or chips, I know in casinos it's all done with chips, but he has piles of chips: red, white, blue, yellow, stacked up like freshly unveiled games of Jenga. Women with large breasts surround him, and their breasts are feathered, like peacock breasts, and they smile and pat his hat, the same one he's wearing now.

"Do you have any *idea* what it does for you in blackjack?" he asks, nervous. "I taught mine to count cards. Forget about it. Six hundred is a bargain. You're too young to gamble, but I'm sure you can work something out some other way." Finally, he looks me in the eyes and smiles, his front top teeth a row of gold shingles, like a zipper in his mouth. "It's the greatest thing on earth. It's the only way to live. Go where I told you. Get one."

eighteen

"eBay, huh?" Dad asks as I sit at the computer in the dining room. I don't want to be distracted by porn sites while I'm looking for squips, so I'm here. Dad puts a hand on my shoulder. "eBay is just amazing, isn't it? You know who would have loved it? Ben Franklin."

Dad has this thing about Ben Franklin (for Ben Franklin?). Give him any technology—the Internet, the postal service, Seeing Eye dogs—and he'll go off on how if only Ben Franklin were alive today, he would be overjoyed to see it and use it, because Ben Franklin was a "forward thinker."

"Ol' Ben just wouldn't have been able to believe it, this entire worldwide community of individuals safely and happily trading their wares. I think he would have loved it even more than air conditioning, which would have been one of his favorites." Dad eats peanut butter with a potato chip. I don't know what to say.

"So what are you looking for? Hmm . . . Beanie Babies?"

"Yeah. That's right." It turns out there's a Beanie Baby named "Squip" (a small, blue squid) so when I typed *squip* in the eBay search box, I got, like, sixty Beanie Baby listings, all for the same stupid doll. Now with Dad leaning over my shoulder assuming that I'm looking for Beanie Babies, I have to legitimize myself by typing "Beanie Baby" in the search box and sitting back for all 9,781 results. Each Beanie Baby is listed as, for example, "2000 Holiday Teddy Bear MWMT," where MWMT indicates that the animal is "mint with mint tag" so you know precisely what kind of lemming or snail it is. Most listings also assure a "smoke-free environment" for the Beanie.

"Seriously, are you gay, son?"

I click through the Beanie Babies—when will he leave? "I'm just looking for something, Dad."

"You lookin' for something at that dance last night, too?" Dad puts his hand on the wall, leans close. "Looking for some *poonanti*?"

"I'm sorry, what?" I stare at the bridge of Dad's nose.

"You know what I mean, Jeremy."

"Well, um, I guess . . . but no. No 'poonanti' last night, Dad."

"Hmm." He straightens up, gesticulates. "You want some, though, don't you? Don't you have that *drive*?"

I grunt. It's not a manly grunt—more like a grunt/sigh. Dad disapproves.

"You know, you're a real depressed kid, you know that?" He turns away, pacing. "Back in the eighteen hundreds, any kid as surly as you, his father would take him to the whorehouse and that would be the end of it. The kid would come back grinning. The madams, they were very familiar with the process— they'd make sure young men got girls with no diseases who'd show them how to perform."

I'm ignoring Dad. This tie-dyed Jerry Garcia Beanie Baby is worth $71! How did these things get so expensive? I knew there was a craze years ago, but I thought it had died out.

"Don't you know your Aunt Linda has, like, ten thousand of those things?" Dad asks.

"Really?"

"Yeah. She's got a whole atticful. Hang out with her more often. Keep her away from me." He smiles.

"Does she have the expensive ones?" I re-sort the Beanie Babies by price: $9,999.99 for a lot of 1,600.

"Jeremy, c'mon, you can't expect me to know too much about stuffed cats—oh, Miller Time."

Yeah, Dad actually says "Miller Time" when he decides to get a beer before watching a football game (college only, "less steroids"). He leaves for the kitchen; I continue the search for a real squip. I can't find anything, but *damn* there's a lot of money in

Beanie Babies: $8,500 for 252 Nectar the Hummingbirds ("I am a full-time Beanie dealer and investor who sells worldwide. This is NOT my hobby. This is how I try to earn a living and support my four children. . . . There are whole states in this country where you won't find 252 NECTAR! THAT'S BECAUSE I HAVE THEM ALL!"), $222 for ten Mom-E Bears. It's insane. I note which Beanies are most popular—any kind of actual bear is a big draw, as are creatures sponsored by hotels or baseball teams. I used to be into baseball cards, so I slip easily into this world of collectibles, this mentality where the only thing that's important is the planet you control and analyze and understand. I look at Beanie Babies for an hour. For the first time all day, I don't think about the squip.

When Mom gets home, I ask her if Aunt Linda might be interested in having me come by to clean her gutters, which I promised to do last year, but forgot. Mom asks why—I tell her it's because I'm a nice guy who loves my family. She gets in touch with Aunt Linda and we make arrangements for next week.

nineteen

"Jeremiah!"

I'm at Aunt Linda's on a Sunday afternoon. In my back pocket, next to the ratty and overused Humiliation Sheet from Friday (a bad day, but I found out Christine's favorite band is Portishead and we talked about that at rehearsal, since Jake wasn't around), there's a list of Beanie Babies I'm after. I hate my aunt and no matter how you slice it, I'm going to need some money to buy a squip. It's not right, but it is, really.

"Come in!" Aunt Linda ushers me through the screen door. She's Mom's sister; her husband, Ray, isn't around, since he's a fire watcher in Montana— he'd rather sit alone in a giant tower and look for forest fires ten hours a day than live with Aunt Linda.

"Oh! Oh!" *Click. Whirr.* She takes a picture of me shambling through her kitchen. "There goes the young handyman! My gosh." *Click.* She's got pictures of me vomiting, pictures of me naked peeing in pools . . . they all go on her refrigerator. "My darling nephew! Would you like some peach-ade?"

"No thanks, Aunt Linda."

"Okay, well, you tell me if you change your mind."

"I will. So should I go upstairs now?" I shift back and forth on the balls of my feet.

"Jeremiah! My goodness! You're not going to *talk* to me? Look, I'm practically an old woman! I want to hear all about your school and your family and your handsome father. . . ." Aunt Linda pulls a stool up to the kitchen table and motions for me to sit on the milk crate that her cat Hiroshima is currently occupying. "Tell me, tell me!"

I sit on the crate, scooch up to the table. I can feel the skin of my butt being stamped into a checkerboard pattern. "Well, I hate school, Aunt Linda."

"Really?"

"Yes. I'm not Cool and I can't get with any girls. So I'm going to be purchasing a supercomputer that will reside in my brain and tell me how to be Cool all the time."

"Oh, goodness." Aunt Linda flips her wrist at me, her orange hair twitching under the shade-filtered light. "You are such a comedian, Jeremiah. Have you ever thought about doing standup?"

"No."

"My husband, God bless him wherever his skinny

ass is, would have made the most terrible standup comedian. But I would have been quite excellent."

"Huh."

"I'm too old now, of course." Aunt Linda smiles. "Do you have a girlfriend?"

"No."

"Now, why *is* that, Jeremiah?"

"I don't know. Can I please clean your gutters now?"

"Let's talk more about you not having a girlfriend."

"Let's not."

"My my. Testy testy." My aunt gets up and paces around her table, then pulls a long metal pole out from behind her refrigerator.

"Let's see how you like this, huh, testy boy!" She starts poking me with the pole! She's six feet away jabbing it at me! It looks like there's tetanus on that pole! I get up very quickly.

"Aunt Linda!"

"Oh, I'm just having a little fun." She pokes again, then stands with the pole at her side, like a pygmy.

"Ahm, I really think I should go up and take a look at your gutters now."

"All right, Jeremiah, you take yourself upstairs." Aunt Linda jabs more as I move out of the kitchen and up to the second floor of her house, which smells like the rim of a big bottle of milk. On the second floor—she still has that spear—I mount a thin stepladder that's attached to the ceiling by, like, one screw from the 1950s and clamber through a trap door into the attic.

"You okay up there?" Aunt Linda asks from below, her face a fat pudding pie.

"Yep."

"You know what you have to do?"

"Go outside and clean the leaves out of your gutter?"

"Yes! Get to it like a good boy. And behave yourself!" Aunt Linda shakes her pole at me—I think it used to be part of an outdoor clothes-hanging apparatus. I close the trapdoor on her fearsome image. God.

I find a pull-down switch and light up the attic. It's not like I have to look hard: sitting on a pyramid of newspapers by a pile of *Time* magazines are a couple of hundred Beanie Babies. I pull the list out of my pocket and start cataloging.

Nectar the Hummingbird! A *full* set of Asian Pacific Bears! This is the frickin' motherlode! I can't believe it. I grab enough Babies to net a clean $500 on eBay—that's enough, I can furnish the last $100 myself—and carry them, cradling them in my arms, over to the attic window. Now comes the tough part: getting the Beanies out and nestling them into the lone tree in Aunt Linda's yard, where I can climb up and rescue them later. Ideally, I'd rather not have them fall to the ground and lie there for any period of time . . . that's sure to downgrade their value.

I press my back against the window and use my coccyx to work it open. Maple is the first to go; I give him a light toss about 15 feet and he lands right in a crook of the tree, as if he were having sex with it. I'm awesome. I throw out Nectar the Hummingbird, the Patriot LF bear, Prickles the Hedgehog, and Prinz von Gold, but I'm not as lucky with them; they fall right to the grass below. I hope Aunt Linda doesn't notice any bear suicides from her kitchen window; I bet not; she's probably torturing Hiroshima with her pole/Jeremy goad.

Once I get the desired Beanies vacated, I clamber through the window and hoist myself onto the roof. It's beautiful up here; any time you can get high in New Jersey it's beautiful because the country is so flat, you can see everything—or at least, Piscataway. It looks natural, like Mother Earth intended for Jersey to be colonized by suburbanites. She grew roads and power lines to welcome us. The tops of her trees and our houses mesh like lichen.

I turn to the gutters; they're less pleasant, filled with leaves so old and black they look like they came from the bottom of a lake in a horror movie. There's no way I'm touching them with my hands, so I pull off a shoe and use it to dredge them up and push them down to the lawn below, making sure no leaf refuse hits my Beanie Babies. *Plat plat plat*. It's forty minutes of numbing work and then I'm done, with the sun setting on me and me sitting on the aluminum siding, taking a drag from an imaginary cigarette. I'm accomplished.

I get back through the window, avoid Aunt Linda as best I can, say my good-byes, and make off with a backpack full of Beanie Babies. (I have to duck down and walk like an army commando when I pass the kitchen window so she won't see.) Once Mom picks me up, everything is secure, and I've even managed to take a digital photo of the Beanies sitting on a bush for my eBay sales shot. Mom asks me how it went, and I tell her I'm always cool with doing family stuff.

twenty

Even without the squip, a week later I discover one way to be Cool—walking around with lots of money. Heading into the Menlo Park Mall with $640 in Beanie Baby-derived cash (more than expected! I put them online Saturday, priced them to move by Tuesday, got payment Wednesday, got the eBay ATM card Friday, withdrew the money Saturday) I feel like Jake Dillinger must feel when he strides across the lawn to Christine's house, knowing he's going to get some. I'm in control of everything. Even if I don't find a squip at this Payless Shoes, at least I'll have wised up to the joys of sauntering around with lots of cash.

Michael drove me here; he's off in HMV listening to music in one of those kiosks where one of the buttons (or headphones) is always busted. I head to the first Payless Shoes I can find: no customers, briskly over-air-conditioned, no attendants to help you try shoes on, and that familiar '80s black-yellow-and-orange Payless color scheme. There's one cashier, an Asian teenager. This might be it!

"Hi, I'm looking for Rack," I approach.

"Yeah."

"You're him?"

"Yeah."

"Hey."

"Hey."

Rack has the Asian Wolverine haircut with the two oversize bangs, bleached, hanging down across his eyes; his hair is short and buzzed in the back. He's probably eighteen, although I tend to think kids my age are eighteen because I have such a warped self-image; he could be fifteen. He's not from Middle Borough, though; I'd have him cataloged.

"Yeah, hi, um, I got sent here by, ah, the . . ." Jesus, I never got the guy's name. "By the *guy* over at B. Bowl-Town lanes. You know who I mean?"

"Oh yes." Rack smiles, polishing a shoe. "My cousin. So you're looking for a squip, right?"

"Yeah." I bite my lip, duck my head into my neck, wary.

"Well, do you have the money?"

"Sure." I grip the wad tightly in my pocket.

"What's your name, then?"

"Jeremy."

"Well, all right, Jeremy. I'm gonna be your guide today. C'mon." Rack gives a well-toothed grin, shakes my hand, and opens a gate that I didn't even know was a gate in the Payless countertop. I step through into his world: exotic topless calendars on the inside of shelves that hold shoe polish and extra laces.

"The squips got moved in back with the legit merchandise," Rack explains. "We got a bunch of new ones in and we've had lots of people asking for them so we had to secure them, y'know? Let's walk." We leave the counter unattended and venture back into the Payless inventory hangar, full of shoes in boxes that lack the insignias and celebrity faces that get you to buy them in the first place.

"Stop," Rack says, removing a totally nondescript Reebok box off the particular nondescript shelf we're at. The back of this Payless is really *big*; it stretches to an indoor horizon like the hallway of my school.

"Take a look." Rack opens the box; inside, padded with tissue paper, are half a dozen gray pills.

"Nice, aren't they?" Rack shakes his head. Then he adopts a more serious pose. "Okay, just so you know: squip is untested technology and obviously it's not exactly legal, which is why you're paying for it with cash in the back of a shoe store. I take no responsibility—neither does my cousin or Payless or anybody else—for what it will do to you. Even if you *could* spit it out and get a refund, there wouldn't be one."

"Understood."

"Let's see the money."

I try my bargaining skills a little. Rack never mentioned a price, so instead of pulling $600 out of my pocket, I select $500 with the sweaty tips of my fingers, pushing seven of the twenties aside. Maybe that'll be enough. I give it to him—so thick.

"Wow, man, you don't need to give me this much." He smiles.

"Really?"

"No, actually, you do." Rack clenches with laughter, pinches a squip from the box and holds it in one hand with my cash in the other.

"Gimme!" I grab. Rack holds it above his head, grins—a return to grade school, a game of keep away.

"Calm down, dude, calm down. What do you want to take your pill with? I've heard people say that if you drink Mountain Dew, it works best."

"Fine!" I hold my hand out. "Whatever."

The pill plops in my hand with a gorgeous little pat. "Here," Rack says, "I just happen to keep some Dew behind the Tevas." He reaches back and pulls out a bottle of incredibly flat, green quasi-soda. I put it to my mouth and swig it—it coats my teeth in a thick sugar film. Ugh. Nasty. But . . . *dun da da dunh da dunn dunn . . .*

The pill goes down.

PART 2

squip

twenty-
one

"What now?" I lean against a Payless shelf. "What's happening?"

"I dunno." Rack lounges on a step ladder and lights up a cigarette. "You hear anything yet?"

I shake my head.

"Well, it's warming up. It'll start soon."

I picture the pill in my stomach, opening like a cocoon, allowing the tiny (invisible?) computer inside to pass through the pinched gate of my duodenum into my intestines and mush its way through my intestinal walls into my bloodstream and shoot its way up to my brain to my neurons (bio class) to start talking to me. What kind of computer is it? How does it work, exactly?

"Do you have one?" I ask Rack.

"Of course." He drags his cigarette lazily.

"Is it on right now?"

"Sure is. It just said you were a chump, but I don't think so."

"Wow. Did yours get you a girlfriend?"

"Man, that's the first thing it does, is get you a girlfriend. I bet yours is working on that right now."

"That's what I want."

Rack nods, rolls his eyes.

Ting.

Whoa. Here we go.

Welcome to SQUIP 2.5.

It's a voice, in my head, but it isn't all that strange. It's like my own voice, but deeper, older, more authoritative. It sounds like—

"Keanu Reeves?"

"Yeah! You're hearing it?" Rack stands up.

"It's *Keanu Reeves's* voice?"

"Sure, but that's just the default." Rack swishes his cigarette, explains. "You can set it for Sean Connery, Jack Nicholson, Tyrese; you can even give it a sexy female voice if you want, but I find that distracting."

SQUIP 2.5 calibration and access procedure in progress.

"*Aaaaaagh!*" Pain like a motorcycle races through my head. "Jesus! *Agh!*"

"It's okay!" Rack puts an arm around me. "It only happens once. It's picking out information from your brain."

"Oh my God . . ." It's like nothing I've ever experienced, transcendent pain, from temple to temple, death, fear, agony, like a spike bent through my ear . . . and then it's over.

HELLO, JEREMY.

"Hey. Ugh."

PLEASE. DO NOT TALK TO ME OUT LOUD.

"It's working!" I tell Rack.

YES, IT IS WORKING. "IT" HAS A LOT OF WORK TO DO, BY THE LOOK OF THINGS.

"It's *working*!" I grin.

"Welcome to the world," Rack says. I expect a hug from him or something, but all he does is get up, crush his cigarette underfoot and lead me back, past monoliths of shoes, to the Payless retail area. A girl is waiting by the cash register.

"Excuse me, is there a reason nobody's attending to customers in here?" she asks, hair bouncing against her cheek, indignant.

TARGET FEMALE INACCESSIBLE DUE TO INTEREST IN OTHER PARTY, the squip declares.

"I'm really sorry, miss," Rack says. He smiles like he can't help it. "But I don't know why you're here. You have nicer shoes than we stock anywhere in this place."

"Well," the girl says. "I'm not looking for me; I'm looking for my boyfriend. He *refuses* to get new shoes—"

"Would you like a cigarette?" Rack asks.

"You can't smoke in the mall!" she whispers.

"Well, you can't, but you can, sort of, in Payless. I won't get you in trouble, I promise."

"Okay," she says, suddenly in on something. Rack makes eye contact and I understand: *I got this girl. Thanks for your money and get out.* I open the gate in the sales counter unnoticed, leave Payless, and walk into the Menlo Park Mall alone—well, sort of alone.

twenty-two

YOU NEED A NEW SHIRT. BUY A NEW SHIRT.

"But I—"

DO NOT TALK TO ME OUT LOUD, JEREMY! THAT IS
RULE NUMBER ONE.

Right. I stand stock-still by an Annie's Pretzel cart.
This is weird.

NO, IT IS NOT. THIS IS WHAT YOU HAVE ALWAYS
WANTED. JUST WALK AND THINK TO ME AT THE SAME
TIME, OKAY? LIKE TELEPATHY.

I always thought telepathy was cool. Like
X-Men.

RIGHT. IT IS COOL. AND NOW YOU GET IT.

Rockin'.

ROCKIN'? IT IS GOING TO BE DIFFICULT TO GET YOU
UP TO SPEED, JEREMY.

Why?

BECAUSE YOU ARE A SERIOUS DORK, JEREMY. SOME
SQUIPS HAVE IT EASY. THEY HAVE TO MEMORIZE

INFORMATION FOR TESTS OR SMOOTH OUT OCCUPATIONAL CHALLENGES OR HELP PEOPLE WITH STUTTERING PROBLEMS. YOU, HOWEVER, DESIRE A COMPLETE BEHAVIORAL OVERHAUL. CORRECT? YOU HAVE TO BE MORE CHILL—

You mean, I have to chill out.

NO, I DO NOT MEAN "CHILL OUT." WE ONLY USE SQUIP-APPROVED DATA FOR THE VERNACULAR, JEREMY. YOU HAVE TO TALK AS PER RAP-SLASH-HIP-HOP, THE DOMINANT MUSIC OF YOUTH CULTURE.

Okay.

NOW, THERE ARE MANY ASPECTS TO THE CHANGES YOU DESIRE AND IMPLEMENTING THEM WILL BE COMPLEX.

Uh-huh. I'm walking back and forth between two indoor trees, not caring how crazy I look.

STEP ONE IS THAT YOU STOP PACING AND GET A NEW SHIRT, JEREMY.

Okay. Okay. I put both hands in my pockets and walk toward Advanced Horizons, one of Menlo Park's Cool clothing places.

HOW COME YOU USE CAPITAL C FOR COOL?

Well—I'm starting to get a little bit comfortable with this—because there are different kinds of cool. There are your friends who are just cool people, you know, like laid-back, and then there are the certified popular, dominating, aristocratic Cool People. And then there's the temperature and the jazz period—

No.

No what?

NO, DON'T USE CAPITAL C. YOU'RE MAKING IT TOO DIFFICULT, JEREMY, PUTTING IT ON TOO MUCH OF A PEDESTAL.

Really?

YES. THE PROCESS THAT WE ARE EMBARKING ON IS COMPLICATED BUT IT IS ALSO . . . SIMPLE. WITH CERTAIN MODIFICATIONS TO YOUR DAILY BEHAVIOR YOU WILL BE COOLER THAN YOU EVER IMAGINED AND YOU WILL NOT THINK TWICE ABOUT IT. HUMAN SOCIAL ACTIVITY IS GOVERNED BY RULES AND I HAVE THE PROCESSING CAPACITY TO UNDERSTAND, OBEY, AND UTILIZE THOSE RULES.

All right. Advanced Horizons appears on the horizon to the right.

DO NOT PUT YOUR HANDS IN YOUR POCKETS. TAKE THEM OUT. ARCH YOUR BACK SO THAT YOUR SHOULDER BLADES ARE ALMOST TOUCHING. WALK LIKE THAT.

I do as I'm told. It feels gay.

THE GAYER IT FEELS, THE BETTER YOUR POSTURE. YOU MUST ALWAYS WALK THIS WAY, JEREMY. I WILL STIMULATE YOUR SPINE TO REMIND YOU. YOU ARE TALL; IF YOU DON'T USE YOUR HEIGHT TO THE FULLEST, TARGET FEMALES WILL ASSUME YOU ARE A LOSER AND MASTURBATOR.

But I *am* a masturbator.

WE'LL FIX THAT.

I have $140—you don't want me to spend it all in this store, do you? I push open the doors to Advanced Horizons.

No, you'll need $100 of it later. Let's spend $40 on at least one shirt and if you need more, you can use your mother's credit card.

How do you know about that?

Your brain. I started up with a partial data dump from memory to memory. I know some things.

Well, that card is only for emergencies.

You *are* an emergency, Jeremy.

Inside the store, I walk with a back as straight as I can from aisle to aisle. Each shirt I see, I pull out and inspect, but of course I'm not really inspecting it. The squip is.

No. No. No. No.

You're tough.

No. No.

In the end, the squip approves of two items: a navy-with-gold-trim Shago sweatshirt and an Eminem T-shirt that says I like the pope/the pope smokes dope. (Buy that now; you're going to want Eminem merchandise.) The last of the $40 is obliterated by the sweatshirt and Mom's credit card has to be called in for the T-shirt. I'll need to explain that to her later. Damn.

That is something else we have to work on. How come you don't curse?

I don't know, really. I do sometimes. I guess I don't need to all the time. (I try to interact with the cashier and squip at the same time.)

YES, YOU DO. FIFTY TIMES A DAY YOU HAVE TO SAY ANY COMBINATION OF THESE WORDS: FUCK, ASS, BITCH, SHIT, DICK, PUSSY, DILL-LICKER, HAIRY NECESSARIES—

Whoa whoa whoa. I do not.

WHAT DO YOU MEAN, YOU DO NOT? DO YOU WANT TO ACHIEVE YOUR GOALS WITH FEMALES OR DO YOU WANT TO KEEP JERKING YOUR SKINNY SELF OFF ALL THE TIME? I KNOW THE RULES, JEREMY.

Yeah, but if I talk like that, Christine'll be pissed.

TRUE.

She doesn't want to see me cursing all the time.

GOOD POINT. LET'S USE BLANKED-OUT WORDS, THEN. LIKE EVERY TIME YOU SAY FUCK I'LL PUT IN A _ _ C _ , AND ASSHOLE BECOMES _ _ S _ _ L _ .

Deal. F _ _ _ p _ _ .

I kind of hate Keanu Reeves's voice. Can you switch to, ah, Brad Pitt?

WE COULDN'T GET HIS RIGHTS. YOU SURE YOU DON'T LIKE KEANU?

Uh . . .

C'MON, JUST LISTEN. ISN'T IT SOOTHING?

I guess.

ALL RIGHT THEN, the squip concludes as Keanu. We head through the mall to meet up with Michael. I could see how—

JEREMY, STOP. GET A FROZEN YOGURT.

"I'm sorry?"

GRRRRR.

I mean, I'm sorry?

<small>First change shirts; then get a frozen yogurt.</small>

But I need to meet my friend . . . what time is it anyway?

16:20 <small>hours.</small>

Huh? What?

<small>I default to military time. Would you like standard time?</small>

Sure.

4:20 <small>p.m.</small>

Then I definitely have to meet Michael. I told him—

<small>Jeremy, you do not need to meet Michael *right now*. In fact, I have to explain something to you *right now*. Sit down.</small>

Um—I park my butt on a metal bench by a garbage droid and concentrate. It's unnerving communicating with a disembodied Keanu Reeves. Especially when he's stern.

<small>Your performance in that store was admirable, but too questioning. Your performance now is worse. You need to understand: I am an adviser. Yes?</small>

Okay.

<small>You paid quite a bit of money for me. True?</small>

True.

<small>My advice is not based on this world alone. Due to my quantum structure I am able to interact at a low level with photons in parallel universes and</small>

EXTRAPOLATE FORWARD, KNOWING THEIR ENTANGLED STATES, TO SEE WHAT THOSE UNIVERSES HAVE TO OFFER.

Uh—

RIGHT NOW I AM ENVISIONING A UNIVERSE IN WHICH YOU GET SOME FROZEN YOGURT WITH YOUR SHAGO SWEAT-SHIRT ON AND THINGS TURN OUT WELL FOR YOU.

Okay.

I HAVE YOUR BEST INTERESTS IN MIND, JEREMY. ALWAYS. WHY DON'T YOU EXPLORE THEM?

Okay. I'll give this a shot. I drop into the nearest bathroom. Hoping to look beefier, I stuff the new T-shirt over my current model and put the sweatshirt on over that. Then I head to the combination Mrs. Field's/TCBY facility for yogurt.

EXCELLENT. SEE?

Whoa! Anne is here, from my math class, looking, um, marginally cute. She has little breasts, so she doesn't wear a bra as she snacks on the pointy end of a used cone at her own tall, circular table.

NOW YOU'VE GOT TO APPROACH HER, WITH THAT GOOD POSTURE WE TALKED ABOUT.

Wait, though! I don't like Anne.

WHAT DO YOU MEAN?

I don't like her. I don't *want* to talk to her.

JEREMY, HOW DO YOU KNOW WHOM YOU LIKE AND DON'T LIKE?

That's actually something I've never had a prob-lem with—

LIKING SOMEONE IS A QUANTUM CONCEPT. DID YOU KNOW THAT?

Really.

YES. EVEN BY THINKING THAT YOU MIGHT LIKE A TARGET FEMALE, YOU CREATE AN INFINITUDE OF WORLDS WHERE THAT FEMALE IS MET, COPULATED WITH, AND GIVEN COMPANION STATUS.

Really?

"Jeremy!" Anne pushes a drop of frozen yogurt over her lower lip, into her mouth.

HELLO.

"Hello," I say.

"Well, okay, 'hello,'" Anne responds. She smiles, drapes her hands over the table. It's nice to hear a voice that comes from the outside world, but still, she isn't attractive.

"Do you know Chloe?" Anne continues, and I turn to see *the* Chloe—Hot Girl Chloe, the Chloe with the tail from the dance—sitting in the seat next to Anne's! How the _ _ _k did I not see her? I stare, dumbfounded.

"Hello," Chloe says comfortably. She has on a necklace with "Fun Size" Snickers and Milky Ways hanging off it, just in case I didn't know she was hot.

"I didn't see you," I say.

YEAH, YOU DIDN'T. FUNNY, HUH, HOW YOUR OPTIC NERVES CAN BE BLOCKED TO YOUR ADVANTAGE?

"Do you want a Snickers?" Chloe asks, jutting her breasts and necklace out at me.

"Guh . . . yes." I pull one off her soft neckline. The space between the tops of her breasts and chin looks like a whole continent.

"Chloe and I are taking a break from that crap Mr. Gretch assigned, you know?" Anne uptalks. "Did you do it?"

WE'LL DO IT LATER. IT WILL TAKE SECONDS. IGNORE HER. LET THE FEMALES INTERACT.

"It's not a study break," Chloe turns to Anne, putting her body back in neutral. "You make it sound like a *study break*."

"Oh, yeah. My bad?" Anne covers her mouth with four fingers. Then she turns to me: "So, Shago?" She stifles a laugh. "Isn't that, uh, Lil' Bow Wow's clothing line?"

LIL' BOW WOW IS ACTUALLY CALLED BOW WOW NOW, WITH A SUCCESSFUL MOVIE AND FASHION DESIGN CAREER. THE SHAGO LINE STANDS FOR HIS REAL NAME, SHAD GREGORY MOSS.

"Um, Lil' Bow Wow is Bow Wow now, and Shago is Shagregory Moss," I repeat.

"No way," Chloe slurs from her spot at the table. "How do you know that?"

She waits for me to answer, turning down to the pink yogurt shake that occupies her. She looks at my eyes, I think, but I can't be sure—

Of course she's looking at your eyes. Who else is here? We have to move this along, Jeremy. Put your knuckles on the table like a brute of some kind.

I do. It's a lot easier to do this stuff when you're told to.

Now look toward Chloe, but open your mouth a bit, so your lips show full without revealing your teeth. You need to appear uncaring and very intense, yet meek.

I part my lips.

Now say, "You're a really pretty girl, Chloe. You looked great at that dance."

"You know you're really pretty, Chloe. You looked great at the dance." I can't believe I'm saying it.

"Um . . ." Chloe raises her eyes to mine.

"Maybe we can hang out sometime." Say it like you don't care about your own death.

"Maybe we can hang out sometime."

Chloe . . . Jesus, Chloe is looking right at me!

Don't smile. Stay intense. And don't think Jesus. Think f_ _ _.

F_ _ _.

"Whatever," Chloe finally says.

Whatever? An excellent start. Now say that you're a graffiti artist—

"Jeremy!" Michael yells, rushing into Mrs. Field's/TCBY, exasperated, with his headphones. He doesn't ever look exasperated. Guess I'm popular today. He gasps at my shirt. "Where have you been?"

"Mom's home," Chloe says under her breath. I notice that Michael has bad posture and bad dandruff; it didn't use to be so much worse than mine, but you can see it from across the room now.

BRUSH HIM OFF; WE HAVE BUSINESS HERE.

"Um . . . I'm talking to these girls; what do you want from me?" I ask Michael. And what does he want? A girl, same as me. If he had run into one over by the HMV music kiosks, he'd still be there.

"O-kay," he says, his lips squirming. "Well, um, I'm going now, so if you want that ride home you've got to—"

TAKE A RIDE WITH THE GIRLS.

"Actually, Anne?" I turn, ignoring Michael. Anne looks weirded out by what I just said to Chloe, but she still looks admiring. "You've got a ride outta here, right?"

"Yeah."

"Could I maybe go with you?" My speech is coming out more and more in tune with the squip's suggestions. "My house is right by school."

"Oh yeah," she says. "This girl Jill? She'll totally drive you."

"Okay." I look back for Michael, but he's gone. That was quick. Guess I'll sort things out with him later.

Chloe is sucking loud air out of the bottom of her yogurt shake. She doesn't look at me, but she says, "Guess we're going to be hanging out sooner instead of later, huh?"

twenty-three

Sitting with girls rules. Anne must really like me; she starts badmouthing Jenna as soon as I pull up a stool between her and Chloe and the squip tells me that if a target female is attracted to you, she will complain about things to you. That reminds me of Christine and how *she* started by complaining about Mr. Reyes to me, and I wonder if the squip knows about Christine. I hope so. I hope it saw her in the brain data dump or whatever.

I DID.

Under careful instructions, I dutifully agree with everything Anne says, whether it's about the vileness of Jenna or the merits of Avril Lavigne or the unattractiveness of pierced nipples. ("It's like, they come *out*.") Chloe stays quiet but the squip convinces me—unbelievably—to move my leg under the table so that it's touching hers in a meaty, unmistakable way. Chloe doesn't object! My dick gets hard and it's nice to feel that happen when not in the vicinity of a keyboard.

NEWS FLASH: THE RAPPER EMINEM HAS JUST BEEN DECLARED DEAD FOLLOWING A FREAK STREET-HOCKEY ACCIDENT.

What? (I'm careful not to talk out loud.)

EMINEM HAS DIED. USE IT IN CONVERSATION.

But how do you know he's dead?

THE INFORMATION EXISTS, THEREFORE I AM ABLE TO DETECT IT.

How does that work?

WELL, IT HAS TO DO WITH QUANTUM ENTANGLEMENT AND TELEPORTATION. EMINEM'S BODY HELD ENERGY, IN THE FORM OF PHOTONS. WHEN HE DIED, SOME OF THESE PHOTONS DISCHARGED FROM HIS BODY WITH CERTAIN PROPERTIES THAT WERE DETECTED BY A SQUIP NEAR THE SCENE OF HIS DEATH.

Really?

THIS KNOWLEDGE WAS REFINED AMONG OTHER SQUIPS VIA QUANTUM TELEPORTATION AND THERE ARE LOTS OF SQUIPS IN THIS WORLD, SO IT GOT TO ME WITH ALMOST NO TIME LOSS. BUT WOULD YOU JUST SAY IT? HAVEN'T YOU NOTICED THAT NEITHER GIRL HAS TALKED FOR 7.3 SECONDS?

"Did you ladies hear about Eminem?" I ask. The squip says *ladies* is all right to say; it's "corny but disarmingly distinctive," it says.

"Ugh. I hate him," Chloe says. Heat pulses through her taut calf to my leg. "What happened?"

"He's, um, dead. Eminem died. I read it on the Internet," I lie. "He got busted up in a street-hockey incident."

"No way!" Anne shrieks, standing up and nearly knocking over the table. She stocks herself next to me. "What do you mean 'saw it on the Internet'? Are you joking? That's a lie!"

"No," I say simply, hoping that the squip isn't tricking me. It can't trick me, can it?

No. I can't.

"*Hahgg*—" Anne gasps, face contorted.

"C'mon." Chloe plays with her candy necklace. "You knew he was gonna die sooner or later."

"No . . ." Anne buries her head in my shoulder, to the extent that you can bury anything in something that bony. "I was just listening to him today. . . ." she whimpers. Chloe's leg presses hard against mine.

Notice how the plight of one female produces favorable behavior on the part of the target? the squip asks.

Yeah.

Notice how tragedy brings females to you?

Yes. Is that really true Eminem's dead?

In this universe, absolutely.

"Omigosh, what's wrong?" A voice streams in from the entrance to Mrs. Fields/TCBY. It's a tall blond; this must be Jill, the older female with driving qualifications who's assigned to take us all home.

"Eminem's d-dead!" Anne sobs.

"What? No way!" Jill spits.

"Jeremy told us," Anne continues.

"Who's Jeremy?"

"Me! I'm Jeremy."

"You? Who are you?"

"He's from my m-math class?" Anne uptalks as if it's her only comfort. "He saw it on the Internet?"

"Whoa, serious?" Jill raises her eyebrows. "That is *messed* up."

We all pause, think about our own deaths, I guess.

"Well, let's get to the car and we'll listen to Hot 97 and they'll say if it's really happened or not," Jill says, challenging me. She's built like a deer, or Britney Spears, who looks very deerlike.

"Okay," Chloe gets up slowly. "I can't wait to hear how exactly that hockey stick or puck or whatever got nailed to his skull."

"Hockey stick?" Jill asks.

All four of us get up—me and three girls, what a surprise—and strut out of the Menlo Park Mall to Jill's car. My leg feels cold where Chloe no longer touches it. When we get in the vehicle, Jill flips on the radio before the engine even turns over. No news—just the usual R&B about getting married mixed with rap about shooting prostitutes. I sit in back with Chloe as one song ends and the DJ comes on with a slightly different tone than his usual guttural grunting.

"Yo, yo, all—news from up the street. We are just getting word—break it to y'all first, knowhumsayin', news you are not going to get anywhere else and you might not believe. . . ." He goes on, with the aid of more clauses, to announce that Eminem has indeed died after being sticked in the face outside a Detroit Chuck E Cheese. As he says it, Chloe turns to me, reapplying her leg on almost exactly the spot she blessed before.

"You're psychic, aren't you?" she asks. Her lips part.

No, just in the loop.

"No, I'm just in the loop."

Chloe bites her lip. At this point my dick hurts from a 45-minute battle with my pants.

Ask if you can get her phone number so you can hang out sometime.

"Chloe, can I get your number so we can hang out sometime?"

"Uh-huh." She nods, but doesn't move her eyes from my face as I reach for my cell phone (Mom gave it to me, prepaid, only for emergencies; no one ever calls) to record the number.

Let's not be employing Stone Age technology. I'll track the numerics.

"Don't you need something to write it on?" Chloe asks as I converse with the squip.

"No, I'll remember," I reassure.

"Really? That's weird."

"What do you think I have to remember that's more important than your number?" I ask.

VERY NICE. YOU'RE GOOD!

Chloe smiles. Then she gives me the number.

"Okay—I mean, *cool*," I rumble, instantly forgetting each digit. I hope the squip did its job.

I DID.

Ten minutes later Jill leaves me off at my house. Six eyes watch me like a demigod as I step from the car. I'm not just a dork now; I'm a psychic dork with a Shago sweatshirt. And Chloe's phone number.

YES. YOUR CHUMPINESS IS BEING REMEDIED. NOW LET'S WATCH SOME TV SO I CAN GET MORE INPUT ON THIS UNIVERSE.

twenty-four

"Michael called," Mom says as I pass like butter through the bikes and old furniture that clutter the hall.

DEAL WITH HIM LATER.

"I'll deal with him later." I go to the bathroom and void myself.

LET'S SEE WHAT WE HAVE TO WORK WITH DOWN THERE.

My eyes roll south.

HMM. UNCIRCUMCISED.

Well . . . yeah. Wouldn't you know that from accessing my brain before or whatever?

I LEARNED THE BASICS OF YOUR QUANTUM STATUS IN THIS UNIVERSE, JEREMY. I LEARNED HOW MUCH MONEY YOU HAVE AND WHETHER OR NOT YOU WERE GAY. I'M STILL GETTING FILLED IN ON DETAILS.

What if I *were* gay?

I'D TEACH YOU HOW TO MEET GUYS. IT'S EASIER.

Huh.

LET'S FOCUS BACK ON YOUR GENITALS, THOUGH. LOTS OF FEMALES DON'T LIKE UNCIRCUMCISED MEN. DID YOU KNOW THAT?

No. I mean—

YOU MIGHT WISH TO CONSIDER A REMEDY, IN THE FUTURE.

Like get circumcised? That's crazy—

NO PROTESTS. JUST SOMETHING TO THINK ABOUT IF THE POSSIBILITY ARISES FINANCIALLY. LET'S GET A READ ON THE REST OF YOUR BODY. TO THE MIRROR.

I walk to the bathroom mirror and take off all my clothes, including my triple layer of shirts.

LOTS OF WORK, JEREMY, LOTS OF WORK.

Why?

YOU SEE HOW YOU LOOK SORT OF SKINNY AND NORMAL?

Yes.

WE CAN'T HAVE THAT. DEFINED ARMS, BUT NO PECS, ENTIRELY UNEXTRAORDINARY. YOU ALSO NEED TO WAX YOUR CHEST.

But there's no hair on my chest!

EXACTLY. WE'LL KEEP IT THAT WAY. TO THE TELEVISION!

I dress and walk out of the bathroom, curious and fearful about something. Hey, is there any way to turn you off?

Silence.

Nothing! No voice in my head. What happened?

RIGHT HERE.

Okay, so if I want to turn you off, I just *think* about you being off?

OR YOU SAY "SHUTDOWN"; I'M NATURAL-LANGUAGE CAPABLE.

I plunk down on the couch and flip on the cable.

WHAT IS THAT OBSTRUCTION?

That's my Dad's Bowflex.

WELL, MOVE IT.

Huh. Good idea. I get up and move it. The cable is preset to the Discovery Health Network for Mom and there's a doctor talking: "The acid in the stomach is so acidic that it is more acidic than the most acidic jalapeño." What the hell is this? I flip to *Dismissed*.

EXCELLENT. LET'S TAKE A LOOK AT HOW THESE ATTRACTIVE AND POPULAR INDIVIDUALS INTERACT. ALSO, I NEED TO SEE WHAT SORT OF FEMALES I LIKE.

Excuse me?

I KNOW ABOUT YOU, JEREMY, BUT I KNOW LITTLE ABOUT THE WOMEN THAT POPULATE YOUR UNIVERSE. I NEED TO SEE THEM SO I CAN MAKE DECISIONS ABOUT WHICH TYPES TO TARGET FOR MAXIMUM STATUS.

Well, I already know which girls I like.

OH, YOU DO? SO YOU WOULD PREFER TO STAY CONSTRAINED TO YOUR PREFERENCES?

Uh, yeah. I really dig this girl *Christine*—

JEREMY, LOOK.

What?

LOOK AT THE MEN ON TELEVISION.

This episode of *Dismissed* has two guys in bathing suits pawing at a girl with blond pigtails. I don't get it.

LOOK AT THEIR BODIES.

So?

THEY LOOK NOTHING LIKE YOURS, JEREMY. THEIR PECS ARE ON AVERAGE 1.4 INCHES MORE PRONOUNCED THAN YOURS. THEY ALSO POSSESS MORE DEFINED ABDOMINAL MUSCLES. IN PARTICULAR, THE SARTORIUS, WHICH SEPARATES THE ABS FROM THE TOPS OF THE THIGHS, IS VERY CONSPICUOUS. SEE THAT CLEAR V DENOTING SEXUAL READINESS?

Well.

WELL, WHAT DO YOU EXPECT TO DO ABOUT THAT, JEREMY? DO YOU THINK THAT YOUR BODY IS GOING TO CHANGE ON ITS OWN? TO ACCESS FEMALES LIKE THE ONES ON THIS PROGRAM, WHO ARE CLEARLY MORE ATTRACTIVE THAN ANYTHING YOU HAVE STORED IN MEMORY, YOU NEED TO CHANGE YOUR BODY COMPLETELY.

You mean, like, work out?

YES. LIKE, WORK OUT. IN FACT, WE MIGHT WANT TO DERIVE A SYSTEM FOR WORKING OUT.

"How is everything in there?" Mom asks from the dining room, behind her curtain.

"*Muh,*" I answer.

WHAT IS YOUR FAVORITE FOOD, JEREMY?

Double Delight Oreos with Peanut Butter 'n Chocolate Crème, I answer. That's easy.

Okay.

With milk.

Obviously. So let's try something.

What?

Keep your peanut butter oreos by the TV. Whenever you see someone with a built, healthy body on any program, like right now, you do a push-up. Whenever you see someone with a sort of large, palsyish head like yours and a skinny paper body like yours, you eat a cookie. Then I can watch TV all the time and fill your mental banks with motivating girl types and you—you will notice a change.

Okay. I do as I'm told. I find quickly that when you watch TV with these restrictions, you eat so few cookies and do so many push-ups that you might as well just lie on the floor. So I do. Mom comes in and I'm down there huffing away to *The E! True Hollywood Story: American Gladiators.*

"Jeremy! I'm impressed."

"Yeah," I answer.

I get buff in two weeks.

twenty-five

But I don't want to get ahead of myself. That night, in my bedroom, when I jiggle the mouse to wake the computer, the squip has something to say.

STOP MASTURBATING.

Right. I forgot this was one of your policies.

AREN'T YOU TIRED FROM THE PUSH-UPS?

Not so tired that I can't talk to girls online.

JEREMY, IF YOU'RE NOT TOO TIRED TO KEEP FROM MANUALLY STIMULATING YOURSELF, YOU MUST DO MORE PUSH-UPS. WOMEN CAN *TELL* IF YOU MASTURBATE AND IT CASTS A BAD LIGHT ON YOUR APPEARANCE. ALSO, MANY OF THE "GIRLS" YOU TALK TO ONLINE ARE ACTUALLY MEN WITH MAJOR PHYSICAL IMPEDIMENTS—

Shutdown.

There it goes. Silence. It's nice to take a break. I go online with my pants unzipped and Michael is there, waiting.

"what's up popular asshole?" he says on AIM.

"call me" I say back.

Michael phones. I pick up so quickly, my parents only hear half a ring.

"What's up, popular asshole?" he says.

"Look, I'm sorry man. I just *had* to stick around with those girls, you know?"

"You're a f_ _ _ _ _ _ dick, Jeremy. I drove you to the mall just like I drove you to the bowling alley last week for no _uck_ _ _ reason and you ditched me and ended up talking to *two* cute girls and you didn't give me _h_t. You treated me like a *burden*—"

"Both of the girls weren't cute! Only Chloe was cute."

"I think Anne's pretty cute too, dick! I'll take your castoffs."

"Well." I'm at a loss for words. Startup.

TELL HIM YOU WERE IN A VERY DELICATE SITUATION TRYING TO GET THE PHONE NUMBER OFF CHLOE.

"I was really trying for Chloe's number, dude; you just showed up at the wrong time."

GIVE HIM THE FIVE-MINUTE RAP.

"If you had come by *five minutes later* we would have left together."

"Well . . . did you get her number?"

That's the only thing that's going to make Michael feel better now: my failure. Too bad.

"Heh. Yeah. It's right here." I point to my head. That reminds me, should I call Chloe tonight?

ABSOLUTELY NOT.

"How'd you get her number?" he whines.

"I'm getting slick, man."

"_u_ _." Michael hangs up. He does that a lot. I start to call him back.

NO, the squip says. LET IT GO. YOU DON'T NEED HIM. HE'S UNSTABLE. TOMORROW AT SCHOOL WE'RE GOING TO BUILD YOU A NEW CIRCLE OF FRIENDS.

What? No way. (I keep dialing.)

JEREMY, STOP AND LISTEN TO ME. ADVISER, RE-MEMBER?

I stop.

TOMORROW, YOU ARE GOING TO HAVE ALL NEW PEO-PLE TO DEAL WITH, DO YOU UNDERSTAND?

How?

HOW? HOW DOES ANYBODY DO IT? YOU GET GOOD CLOTHES, WALK IN WITH CONFIDENCE AND SHED UNNE-CESSARY HUMANS. LIKE MICHAEL.

He's not unnecessary—he's my friend.

LISTEN. (The squip can be very soothing when it wants.) YOU'RE NOT LOSING HIM FOR GOOD. JUST PUTTING HIM ASIDE A BIT. ONCE YOU GET YOURSELF SIT-UATED IN THIS NEW SITUATION AND HE CALMS DOWN A LITTLE, YOU CAN MAKE THINGS UP TO HIM BY INCLUDING HIM IN WHATEVER YOU AND YOUR NEW FRIENDS DO. DON'T YOU THINK HE'LL APPRECIATE THAT?

I guess.

YOU TWO WILL FINALLY GET AHEAD IN MIDDLE

BOROUGH, JEREMY. YOU'LL BECOME WHAT YOU ALREADY THINK OF YOURSELVES AS—SMART AND INDEPENDENT-MINDED PARTICIPANTS IN HIGH-SCHOOL CULTURE!

Sh_ _! I totally forgot! What about that work Mr. Gretch wanted? (I put the phone down.)

NOT TO WORRY. SHOW IT TO ME.

I pull out a wrinkled sheet of math problems from my backpack—I lost the textbook for math, so when problems are assigned I have to copy them from someone else's book, usually Michael's. I put the sheet on my desk.

THIS DOESN'T LOOK HARD. MAY I?

Sure. And then something incredible happens. Something revolutionary and perfect that everybody should have the pleasure of experiencing at least once. I look at each problem on the sheet, scanning slowly like one of those expensive scanners that gets really good resolution. For every question I see, the squip tells me the answer instantly; I think it even helps move my eyeballs along at data-entry speed. And these aren't easy problems—they're trigonometry proofs. I'm done with the sheet in thirty seconds.

SEE HOW THAT WORKS?

That's amazing.

WAIT. CHANGE THAT ONE AND THAT ONE. YOU NEED TO MAINTAIN CORRECT PERCENTAGES IN THE LOW NINETIES SO AS NOT TO AROUSE SUSPICION IN YOUR INSTITUTION.

Right. You're amazing. How do you do it?

Quantum principles, Jeremy.

Like what?

Qubit memory, parallel processing. Those things.

What are they? Tell me.

It's easy. Take your desk.

What about it?

Well, something's either on the desk or off it, right? It can't be both at the same time.

Right.

Most things in life are like that. You're either dead or alive. In a car or outside it.

Right.

But then again, there's a whole class of phenomena that don't fit into that either/or classification. You love your mother, but you hate her too. You want to kill yourself sometimes, but you're still a pretty happy kid. Right?

I guess.

Emotions, human dilemmas, planning, writing, relationships—none of these are cut-and-dried. But with normal computers, cut-and-dried ones and zeros are used to represent information. That's called binary code. You see it all the time. Anytime a movie comes out with computers in it, they put a whole string of ones and zeros behind the hero on the poster, correct?

Sure.

So a piece of information in a normal computer can be a one or a zero. That's called a bit. But I don't use ones and zeros; I use photons, tiny pieces of light called "qubits." Each of these qubits can be a one or a zero or a sort of in-between state.

So you have one-halfs instead of just ones and zeros?

Sort of. I have intermediate states that allow me to work in a massively parallel way; I can represent a group of numbers in the same space it takes a normal computer to represent a single number. I work like your brain. But better. And that's why I do your homework instantly.

Yeah. Amazing.

Don't waste those compliments on me. Practice saying that to girls.

"Hi, you're *amazing*," I tell the dull air of my room. Then I laugh.

Getting there.

Let's do some more push-ups.

Sure.

I get going. After twenty reps, with the squip encouraging me and telling jokes, I'm so tired that I roll into bed without thinking about jerking off. My eyes just shut and then . . . bam, I'm in the world of squip-active dreaming. Which rules.

See, I haven't had dreams in years, or at least dreams I could remember, and I've never ever had sex in my dreams, ever, but tonight I conjure up an unimaginable pastiche of women and sex and money. Chloe is there, as is the blonde with pigtails from *Dismissed*, as is Christine, as are the women I saw on TV after *Dismissed*, during my push-ups. There are rich and famous beautiful folks everywhere and I'm talking to all of them, conversing with Keanu Reeves, actually, while Chloe makes out with my ankle (and a chick elf does too, with the other one). The setting is a garden, but the plants are all stringy muscle cells, tendons, and vein-vines, with nerves growing like bleached trees toward the ceiling. And the ceiling is really the apex of my skull and right up there is the gray pill, like the sun, with a smiley face painted on its side. "You are cool, Jeremy," it says, finally moving its lips instead of just thinking to me. "You are *so* cool."

twenty.-
six

I *am* cool. The next day at school I prove it. First the squip tells me I have to wear the "I like the Pope/The Pope smokes dope" T-shirt because Eminem just died. That's all they're talking about on the radio as I walk past Mom.

"Good morning, sweetie," she says in the kitchen. Mom's buried in her crossword. If she doesn't finish it before she has to leave the house, she's a failure. "How are you?"

IGNORE HER. I get milk out of the fridge.

"I said 'How are you'—What are you wearing?" She stands up very quickly. "You cannot go to school with that!"

"Wow, I didn't realize freedom of expression didn't exist in this house." I've gotten pretty good at repeating what the squip says without missing a beat.

"Freedom of expression doesn't exist for minors, Jeremy, which is what you *are*."

Tell her to go f_ _ _ herself.

No!

Then wear a different shirt out of the house and change before you get to school.

Okay. That works. I leave Mom satisfied, wearing an alternate shirt, exit the house, and morph halfway across the field into the Eminem T-shirt, tall grass tickling my chest. I start singing to myself, one of those silly songs I wrote in my head in sixth grade, back when I wanted to be a rock star: "I'm the— I'm the— I'm the— I'm the— I'm the—*man*! *Dun-dun-dun*—"

No singing, please.

No singing?

Yes. It is annoying. If you're going to make music in your head, please make it rap-slash-hip-hop, the acceptable music of youth culture.

How about this: shutdown.

Phew. I keep the tune going as I cross the field. As I approach school, though, I get nervous and turn the squip on. I climb the stairs and Rich is at the top, hanging with a pack of fawning females. "Quality shirt," he says as I approach.

"Hello, Rich," I nod, squip-prompted. I almost wave but the squip tells me that waving is one of the worst things you can do in any social situation; it makes people question your nonretardedness. "What's up?"

"You headed to class?"

"Not in a rush."

"Huh." Rich eyes me closely. Does he know? Maybe he'll be pissed because I went through Rack to get my squip instead of paying him. Maybe he'll want to kick my ass—

DON'T WORRY. WORRYING RUINS YOUR POSTURE. DISPLAY THOSE PECS WE DEVELOPED LAST NIGHT.

I jut my chest out.

NOW WE'LL SETTLE THIS. ASK RICH IF YOU CAN TALK TO HIM ALONE FOR A SECOND.

"Rich, can you come over here one minute? I gotta ask you something." I lead my former tormentor to the other side of the school steps—the girls turn their heads at us like motion-sensitive cameras. Once I have Rich alone, I await instructions.

SAY, "UP UP DOWN DOWN LEFT RIGHT LEFT RIGHT B A START."

"Up up down down left right left right B A start."

Rich's face lights up: "You got one!" He hugs me gruffly; he's a little short for it, but I hug back.

"Yeah, I got one. Is that like their secret code or something?"

"I don't know. They have their own way of communicating with one another; it's pretty complicated. I'm stoked you got yours. But hey . . . where'd you get it?"

"Well—"

REACH INTO YOUR POCKETS.

You want me to give him that other $100?

YES. FINDER'S FEE. BELIEVE ME, IT'S WORTH IT.

"I went and got it through the information you gave me, Rich, so I figured maybe you'd want a little bit of money for it."

"Hell yeah!" Rich puts his hand out. "You're lucky I don't beat your ass for not buying it through me, though." He smiles.

I hand him the money.

"Seriously," he lowers his voice, "thanks a lot. Things are kinda bad at my house."

I nod.

GOOD JOB.

"Let's go back to the girls," Rich says. "I'll introduce you."

Rich leads me back to his cadre of females, arrayed at the top of the steps as if they are waiting for an audition and not for school. It's a group I'm familiar with from afar: Abby and Brooke and Celine plus others, girls with slight but compelling variations on how a teenage girl should look: glitter, eyebrow rings, color contacts, lip gloss I can almost smell from here.

"Everybody, this is my friend Jeremy," Rich proclaims. His friend! Awesome! A bewildering number of hands—although it's really just seven—

get touched by my soft hand as I move around the circle saying hello. "Hi, ladies," I say to all the girls.

I make the mistake of shaking Celine's hand but the squip keeps me in line for the rest of them—I *slap* instead of shaking, to denote sexual readiness. It's a special, slow kind of slap; as my hand leaves each girl's, my fingertips linger just long enough for heat to flow from my eyes to theirs. The squip keeps track of their names but doesn't need to—these are people I've watched and envied since freshman year.

"So . . . everybody hear about Eminem?" submits Tal, a tiny kid, one of the nongirls in the group.

"Ick . . ." Abby pouts.

BE JADED AND PROFANE.

"I heard that s_ i_ yesterday afternoon," I say. "I'm surprised he didn't get a_ _ _u _ _ _ _ to death."

The group chuckles! I never knew making people *chuckle* could feel so good. It's not like some of them chuckle and others talk out of the side of their mouths about me—they all glitter in my humor.

DISMISSED.

"Anybody see *Dismissed* yesterday?" I offer.

"Aw, that was a good one," Rich chimes in.

"Really? You're into that show?" Unbelievable. Maybe my squip and Rich's are teaming up.

YES. MAYBE.

"I'm totally into it—"

"Me too!" Brooke pipes up, getting my attention.

Brooke! Now! Give the former girlfriend story, the squip orders, and I go into a riff that we planned this morning.

"I don't like watching TV, but ever since I got out of this relationship? . . ." I say to Brooke. She nods. "I have to watch *Dismissed* just to distract myself from the pain, you know?" I keep my eyes heavily lidded, like I'm sad or stoned or broken in some way.

"Awww," Brooke looks down. She's not bad looking. No she's not. "Who'd you break up with?"

"Katrina."

"Katrina Lohst?"

"Yeah." That really is Katrina's last name; it's like a cosmic joke—

"You never went out with Katrina!" a shrill, dry voice accuses me from across the circle. It belongs to Ibby—the only thing anyone knows about her is that she got in a romantic situation with a football guy on Middle Borough's staircase and she was on her knees on one step while he was on the step above her and then the entire football team came charging up the stairs and she freaked out and popped off him and slid down on her knees and had to wear knee bandages for the next few weeks. "I don't know what's up with you, Jeremy. Like three days go you *knew* you were a loser and you didn't butt into our conversations and stuff."

RETALIATION, the squip advises before submitting a line.

"Hey, Ibby," I scuff my shoe on school property. "I heard there was this sale on kneepads at Tar-*get*." I pronounce Target with the French ending the way the girls do.

"F_ _k you." Ibby leaves; one of her friends goes with her, but the other girls stay loyal to the cause.

"I don't know what's up with that," I say to the group, squip-prompted again. "It's like some people just prejudge everybody and don't give anyone a chance to be *themselves*, you know?"

"Yeah." Brooke smiles.

"So you went out with Katrina too?" Rich asks me. That makes me wonder if *he* really went out with her, but the squip tells me that it isn't important who did or didn't go out with Katrina in this universe—it gives you status to say it, and it's possible in so many universes, you might as well just say it.

"Only a little," I respond.

"F_ _ _ that c_ _ _ _ _ _ _," Rich spits. The girls jump; Rich was always a great curser, even before he got a squip. "So who's going to class and who's gonna hang with me in the dank and creepy spot?"

"I'm out," says Celine, as are Tal and this girl Jessica from my play. . . . _ _ _k, I totally forgot about the play!

WHAT ARE YOU WORRIED ABOUT? LINES?

Oh, right. Abby and Brooke stick around so it's just Rich, two girls and myself—an illustrious foursome—who make our way to the "dank and creepy spot" to do something dank and creepy. I hope.

twenty-seven

Wow. People are in class right now.

YES, YES. DON'T MUSE SO MUCH. TAKE THE PIECE.

Rich is passing me his pipe because we're smoking pot outside school in some bushes. Who knew the dank and creepy spot would really be this dank and creepy? I can see the bike rack through a hedge and a few kids kowtowing to it, kneeling to lock up their rides as the late bell rings. The late bell! Jeez, how can I ever worry about the late bell again?

JEEZ?

Sorry.

I take the pipe as it's passed to me. I've never smoked pot before—

AND YOU'RE NOT GOING TO NOW. IT IMPEDES COMMUNICATION PARAMETERS.

What do I do, then?

SMOKE NORMALLY; I'LL FILTER THE ACTIVE COMPOUNDS OUT OF THE CAPILLARIES IN YOUR SKULL.

"Jeremy, you crackin' out over there? You gonna hit it or not?"

I pull with my lips, but no smoke comes into my mouth. IT HAS A CARB. PUT YOUR FINGER OVER THAT LITTLE HOLE. I do, then pull again. It works. I pass to Brooke, sitting cross-legged next to me, as I exhale carefully away from her face. *Uck.*

So if I can't smoke pot because of you, how come Rich is smoking?

HE'S PROBABLY FILTERING AS WELL. HE HAS TO KEEP UP APPEARANCES. OR HE HAS HIS SQUIP OFF.

That's ridiculous. Do you stop people from drinking, too?

ABSOLUTELY. YOU HAVE TO SHUT ME OFF BEFORE YOU DRINK. I'LL START ORDERING YOU TO KILL PEOPLE.

Really?

POSSIBLY.

"So Jeremy, I've never seen you smoke before," Brooke says, passing to Abby with experienced grace.

DO THE DUST JOKE.

"That's because I'm so busy smoking dust," I say. "You know, PCP? I chief that sh_ _ in a shed outside my house all day and have visions."

"Shut up!" Brooke hits me playfully. "You do *not!*"

"Yeah, he does; I've seen him," Rich nods, hitting. "Jeremy's a madman, this kid." Rich slips an arm around Abby; she blushes. Awww . . .

DON'T YOU THINK YOU'D BETTER FOLLOW SUIT?

Right, right. I look at Brooke. How to tackle this? There are so many parts of a girl's body and they're all so compelling. Do I put a hand on her leg?

No. Sit close to her so your legs are touching.

I comply.

Now put your hand behind her and start tracing your fingers up and down her back.

This is impossible; this is impossible; this is not something I could ever do, but I look over at Rich and he's already doing it so what the _ _ck, I do it. I put an arm behind Brooke and smile at her and she smiles back as I touch the little womanly dent between the side of her back and her hip. Then I start to trace up and down.

"That's nice," she whispers.

"Jeremy!" Rich barks. "You want this?"

"No," I say without looking at the pipe. Brooke shakes her head too. My fingers curl and uncurl on her back. Keep looking her in the face. You're doing fine. Her eyes are pretty, green I think, and one strand of hair has fallen over them. Now lean in. You've got this. You've got this locked up. My body leans forward tiny degree after tiny degree and there I am, with my lips wetting themselves on Brooke's, kissing. My first kiss!

Don't mess this up! Part her lips slowly with your tongue. Have your hand grab her back. Don't let it just rest on her. You're the man; you have to lead this.

Gosh, people's mouths taste so *weird*. It's like, well, I guess I expected Brooke's to taste better than mine or at least different. You get used to the way your own mouth tastes and you get so obsessed about other people's that when you finally get to one, you think it'll taste like *something*, something beside pot smoke, you know, like chocolate maybe? Her tongue traces lines on mine and I put my other hand on her leg, just holding it there, trying to put my tongue in deeper.

DOING OKAY, DOING OKAY. RUB HER BACK.

Damn! Brooke's mouth is big! Now it's all the way open and I'm in there licking away—it's like a never-ending cave! Wow!

WOULD YOU SHUT UP AND CONCENTRATE?

Brooke's hands are in my hair; I hope my dandruff isn't attacking her too much. I open my eyes, which have been closed the whole time—not because I was told to close them, just naturally—and her eyes are open too, curious, twinkling. We both laugh and pull apart at our accidental eye contact. Then we keep kissing.

"*Mgmmmph*," she says.

TAKE YOUR TIME, the squip says. BUT IN SIXTY SEC-ONDS YOU'RE GOING TO WANT TO START TOUCHING HER BREASTS. OTHERWISE SHE'LL GET OFFENDED.

Okay. Brooke has very small breasts; that was something I noticed back on top of the steps.

THAT'S WHY YOU'VE GOT TO MAKE SURE TO TOUCH THEM. OTHERWISE SHE'LL FEEL BAD. IT DOESN'T MATTER IF THEY'RE SMALL; WHAT'S IMPORTANT IS THAT THEY HAVE NIPPLES ON THEM. GIRLS LIKE THEIR NIPPLES.

I move my tongue back and forth and up and down and in and out—I even move it a little bit in four-dimensional space, since I take so much time. Heh-heh. I bet I'm moving in 5D space too, like hyperspace, like I'm a hyperspace kisser—

NOW, JEREMY! NOW! NOW!

My hand moves up Brooke's leg to her chest.

FEEL THROUGH THE FABRIC OF HER SHIRT. SEE IF YOU CAN FIND A NIPPLE. IF YOU'RE DOING YOUR JOB, IT SHOULD BE HARD. IT'S ABOUT THE SIZE OF A PENCIL ERASER. YOU KNOW HOW YOU CHEW PENCIL ERASERS IN CLASS? LOOK FOR SOMETHING THAT SIZE.

Assuming that you're going by, uh "stage right," I'm feeling Brooke's right breast. "Oh . . ." she says very quietly, disconnecting herself from my lips. "Oh . . ." It sounds like a bad *oh*, but she's not offering any resistance so I keep palming until a small nub—just like a pencil eraser; good job, squip!—makes itself known by sliding across my hand.

NOW HERE'S THE TRICK. NEVER RUB THE NIPPLES UP AND DOWN. ALWAYS BACK AND FORTH. AND STOP KISSING HER MOUTH. KISS HER NECK.

I comply and Brooke leans back and makes little breathing noises that sound like baby horses with allergies. I use my index finger to rub the unseen but compelling nub back and forth, slowly at first, then really really fast, then kind of fast, then slow and hard, then really really fast again. It's fun.

TIME FOR THE SHIRT TO COME OFF. THEN YOU CAN KISS THE NIPPLES; THAT'S HIGHLY EFFECTIVE. USE YOUR OTHER HAND.

I look back—Rich is lounging on the ground and Abby is licking his belly button, just like Samartha was doing at the dance. That must be his thing. I make some slick squipped eye contact; he understands, leading Abby out of the dank and creepy spot so Brooke and I are alone. I bet he has a backup spot.

GREAT JOB. NOW BOTH HANDS FOR THE SHIRT.

My other hand was in the dirt—pretty useless, huh? I pick it up and pull the lower lip of Brooke's shirt over her navel (with a ring, whoop-de-doo) and then her solar plexus. Finally, in one of those epic moments that I thought only happened on your deathbed, her shirt is up by her neck and her breasts are *splayed out*! Damn! Although they're not really "splayed out," they're more like "laid out," like two little hotcakes from McDonald's with cookies-and-cream nuggets on the top of each one. They are much smaller in person than they were under the shirt; they look like they belong to a ten-year-old. Boy.

"One of your nipples is pierced," I say quietly.

"Yeah," Brooke smiles. "Just got it done."

Go! Go!

I bury my face on Brooke's breast, "stage left" this time, aiming for the ring. I want to stick my tongue through it, this crazy metal sexy thing—

"Aaaaa! Jeremy! Ow! Stop!"

Uh-oh.

I look up. "What?"

"It's infected! You can't lick it."

"It's infected?" I squint at the nipple placed at the end of my nose. Jesus, it's all purple and yellow around the part where the hoop goes through the skin! And *green*! "Oh man, I'm sorry, what did I do?"

Retreat! Retreat! Disease! Retreat!

I pull my head back; Brooke grabs her shirt in a fist and swishes it over her breasts. "I wasn't sure if—"

You could have *told* us.

"You could have *told* us—I mean, me—I mean, wait." I stand up, brush myself off and then kneel down next to her. "I wouldn't have . . . uh, does it hurt?"

"Of course it hurts, and I just got it; I don't want it to close up. . . ."

Uh-oh. Bad situation here, Jeremy.

"I'm *sorry*, okay?" Brooke says.

Talk to her a little bit. Be kind—

"Brooke, no, *I'm* sorry. . . ." I put my bony arm around her and lie down, pull her with me so she's resting on my stomach and I'm resting on the ground with the pot ash and Starburst wrappers.

GOOD MOVE.

"Maybe, you know, it was a bad idea or whatever. . . ."

"Okay," she says, holding my leg. "It'll be healed soon. You could kiss it later, in, like, two weeks. . . ." She keeps her face on my stomach. After we lie like that for five minutes, I excuse myself and go to class.

GOOD JOB. THAT'S THE WAY TO DO IT. NEVER EVER BE MEAN TO GIRLS, UNLESS THEY'RE UGLY. EVERYTHING YOU DO WILL COME BACK TO HAUNT YOU. SHE'LL TELL HER FRIENDS HOW GOOD YOU WERE AND WE CAN BUILD FROM THERE. THAT NIPPLE REALLY WAS A KICKER; I DIDN'T SEE IT COMING.

Well, I keep seeing the nipple—puffy and rainbowed and skewered, a really sad specimen, worse than anything I've seen on the Internet—in front of my face as I go to class. I turn the squip off in school so I can think about the stuff I used to think about.

twenty-eight

Silence in my head doesn't last long. The squip is back on and very much necessary as I stumble into rehearsal. Recently, I haven't been concentrating much on my responsibilities as Lysander. I need the help.

SO THAT'S CHRISTINE.

We're sitting in the front of the theater—squip's advice. It says that if you're in class or some other mandatory dorky place, you sit in back to show you hate it, but if you're in something you've *volunteered* for, you sit up front to show you're the f_ _ _ _n_ *best* at it. Mr. Reyes is going on about the importance of blocking and physical humor in "the work," which is "the very pinnacle—*maaaaaaaa!*—of Shakespeare's comedies." The squip tells me a faulty squip might be making him talk like that.

I try to stay focused on Christine. Isn't she

pretty? I bet *she* doesn't have an infected nipple.

SHE'S OKAY.

She's two seats to my right, next to Jake; I don't like sitting so close to her in these rows. It's easier to be next to her in a circle, where the curve of our seating lets me eye her without turning my head. Here, I have to actually *look* at her to see her—and she notices.

JEREMY, WOULD YOU STOP WORRYING? YOU DON'T NEED TO LOOK AT HER. SHE'LL HEAR ABOUT YOUR EXPLOITS AND GRAVITATE TOWARD YOU NATURALLY, BECAUSE OF PHEROMONES.

Exploits? I don't know if mouthing a diseased breast counts as an "exploit" . . . and what's a phero—

Ow! Something snaps the back of my neck; I swivel to see Mark Jackson laughing fifteen rows behind me with his Game Boy. All that thumb work has given him some aim with rubber bands or staples or whatever it was. I instinctively reach for my Humiliation Sheet, then remember: the squip made me throw them all away. DON'T BE A COMPLETE SCHMUCK, JEREMY, it had said. THIS ISN'T A SITCOM. NO ONE WILL FIND THOSE "CUTE."

IGNORE MARK. WE'LL DEAL WITH HIM IN A MINUTE. LET ME EXPLAIN ABOUT PHEROMONES.

Okay.

PHEROMONES ARE YOUR BODY'S CHEMICAL SIGNALS.

THEY CAN BE ODORLESS AND COLORLESS, BUT TARGET FEMALES PICK THEM UP. THE MOST COMMON THING THEY DENOTE IS SEXUAL AVAILABILITY. WHEN YOU HAVE ANY KIND OF ROMANTIC ENCOUNTER, LIKE THE ONE WE JUST HAD IN THE BUSHES, YOUR BODY RELEASES ALL SORTS OF "JUST GOT SOME" PHEROMONES THAT FEMALES PICK UP ON. HOW DO YOU THINK GUYS WITH GIRLFRIENDS BECOME SO ATTRACTIVE TO OUTSIDE FEMALES THAT THEY'RE FORCED TO CHEAT? PHEROMONES.

Well, sh_ _! Can't you *make* some of them?

CAN'T. NEXT GENERATION WILL.

Next generation of what? People?

NO, SQUIPS, OBVIOUSLY. I'M 2.5. YOU SHOULD SEE WHAT THEY HAVE PLANNED FOR 4.0.

What about 3?

OH, 3 IS COOL TOO. BUT 4.0 HAS STUFF I CAN'T EVEN TALK ABOUT.

Right.

NOW LET'S DEAL WITH MARK. GET UP AND WALK BACK TO HIM.

Mr. Reyes has finished talking and some of the actors are going on stage to block a scene, so nobody notices me striding to Mark's seat. The squip has a great plan, and I execute it perfectly.

"Hey, Mark, did you shoot some crap at me before?" I ask, standing in the aisle beside his row.

"I don't know what you're talking about," he says. Then snickers. *Grrr.* I walk toward him, climbing over seats. As I get close, the screen on his Game Boy SP starts to shudder, like interference on an old TV signal. My head hurts. YOU'RE GIVING OFF A LOT OF ELECTROMAGNETIC RADIATION. OF COURSE IT'S GOING TO HURT.

I make my voice as menacing as I can, which isn't too menacing, but hey—the squip showed me how to tap into new depths of my vocal cords. "Don't ever f_ _k with me again, Mark," I rumble. His screen is freaking out now. He looks up in total disbelief. I pull back like in the PG-13 movies and clench my fist and bring it down and punch him—in the neck. I meant to hit his face, but uh . . . I hit his neck.

"Ow! _ _ _t!" Mark grabs his neck. I punched as hard as I could, but he's not bleeding or anything! THAT'S BECAUSE YOUR BODY IS INCONSEQUENTIAL, JEREMY. MORE PUSH-UPS. "What the fu_ _ is wrong with you, dude? I didn't *do* anything!"

"What's going on back there, hmmmm?" Mr. Reyes shouts from his stool on stage. "Jeremy?"

I must look a little suspicious, standing over Mark with my fists clenched, panting, with Mark's neck all red. But I look down at the Game Boy SP. The actual game has vanished. It just says, in white on black lettering: DO NOT DICK AROUND WITH JEREMY HEERE OR YOU WILL DIE.

"Nothing, Mr. Reyes!" Mark pipes up, quite chipper. "We're just messing around, that's all!" And then he actually hugs me, the second hug today I've gotten from a former foe; I sit down next to him to make a nice scene for Mr. Reyes. His screen clears and he goes back to playing Kill All People 3.

"Are you some kind of demon or something?" he shudders, not looking at me.

"Nothing like that at all."

Doesn't it rule to have power over small-scale electronics?

twenty-nine

SO IF WE'RE EVER GOING TO GET WITH CHRISTINE, WE'VE GOT TO PREP HER.

Okay.

SHE'S WITH THIS GUY JAKE RIGHT NOW, SO WHAT YOU HAVE TO DO IS POSITION YOURSELF FOR THE INEVITABLE FALLOUT WHEN THEY BREAK UP.

Gotcha.

SO YOU NEED TO BE VERY CUTE.

Check.

ALSO, JEREMY, YOU CAN'T PLAY WITH YOUR TESTICLES THROUGH YOUR PANTS. EVER.

Right. I stop. It's an hour later; I'm sitting at the side of the stage, smack dab in the middle of the most boring part of rehearsal, tilting my plastic seat farther and farther back as the action unfolds. (They're working on chairs with tilt alarms, so you'll never fall off.) It's one of many scenes where Puck gets some instructions from Oberon; there's something compelling about the way Christine delivers that Shakespearean phrasing in a halter top. I don't even know if it is a halter top, because I don't know what a halter top is exactly. But halter top— that's a sexy word.

STOP TILTING YOUR SEAT BACK.

I stop. I'm on in thirty seconds and this scene is fun. I get to lie down as Christine sprinkles me with magic dust; then I have to get up and be in love with Hermia, who's played by this girl Ellen, who I'd really have to be under the influence of magic dust to be in love with. I stand at the edge of the thick curtain and burst on stage when I'm supposed to; Mr. Reyes, of course, is asleep.

" 'Fair love, you faint with wand'ring in the wood,' " I declare. "And . . . and stuff . . ."

"AND TO SPEAK TROTH, I HAVE FORGOT OUR WAY."

" 'And to speak troth, I have forgot our way. . . .' "

"WE'LL REST. . . ."

" 'We'll rest us, Hermia, if you think it good, And tarry for the comfort of the day.' " *Phew.* That wasn't so bad. People give me funny, out-of-character looks as I stumble through the next couple of stanzas. (They might also be giving me funny looks because they've talked with Mark Jackson, who's playing Game Boy SP obediently under a table.) I lie down and wait for Christine to sprinkle me with magic dust—she uses actual sparkles, which I hate, because they don't wash off for, like, a month, but I forgive her.

"'Through the forest have I gone, But Athenian find I none,'" she says, from actual neuron memory I bet. When she leans down over me and says "'Weeds of Athens he doth wear,'" the squip says, *Now!*

"*Rrragh!*" I snap, biting at Christine's nose.

"Jesus!" She pulls back. I stick my tongue out and loll it around, panting under her. "*Hua-hua-hua.*" She smiles at first, then gets deadly serious. "What's wrong with you?" She stares down at me.

I scrunch my eyes up. I have to look cute. "*Grrr?*"

"Mr. Reyes! Jeremy is messing around," Christine tells on me. She frickin' *tells on me*. Reyes wakes up as she elaborates: "He's, um, acting like some sort of dog or animal."

Reyes chastises me: "Get up, young fool! Redo the scene!"

THAT WAS A SUREFIRE PLAN. THIS GIRL'S TOUGH.

Yeah, apparently. I return to the curtain, start the scene over again and do it so many times that by the end of rehearsal I can handle it without the squip. Christine doesn't smile once for the rest of the day and Jake Dillinger isn't too happy either; "Stay away from her," is all he says, with a big hand planted on my shoulder, as I await a run-through by the curtain.

That didn't really work out as planned, huh? I consult the squip as we walk home.

No, it didn't.

I hate rejection. Like, sometimes I wonder why I fear it so much, but then when I meet it head on, I decide that it's good for me to fear it, because I hate it. I hate it with my soul.

It's not that bad. Rejection is entertaining!

No, it's not.

Of course it is. If you view your interactions with females as prospective entertainment, rejection can be just as fun, if not more fun, than gaining access. Once you take that view, you'll be out there looking for rejection, and females will flock to you because of the antifeedback mechanic of pheromones. But that's high-level stuff.

I'll work on it.

In the meantime, you are right. Our cutesy tactics with Christine failed. We're going to try another plan.

What's that?

We are going to get to her by hooking you up with as many girls as possible, making her jealous. And we are going to start with Chloe.

Woo-hoo! Deal.

I jump up in the field and kick my heels together.

Let's never, ever see that again, okay?

thirty

Chloe, Chloe, *dum de dum dum*. I call her with the squip off, testing myself, seeing if I can do it alone. I dial the number, which I eventually stored in my computer under a file called "peeps," in a special way. This was Michael-recommended, way back: first I press the 1, then the 1-7, then the 1-7-3, then the 1-7-3-2, hanging up each time so that the momentum just builds and builds until there I am, connected to Chloe's cell, chatting with a girl whom I used to be afraid to look at.

I forget what day it is, really. The squip keeps track of all that.

"Hi, Jeremy?"

"Yeah, uh, hello, it's—how'd you know it was me?"

"Well, I have everybody's number stored in my celly, so if someone calls and it's a new number, there's very few people it could be, and I figured you would call soon."

"Wow."

"Yeah . . . this number is closely guarded."

"I bet."

"That's a joke, Jeremy."

"*Riiiight.*" I consider trying to laugh, but edit that out. "So what's up?"

"Not much, what are you up to?"

"Jus' chillin'."

"Me too."

"Yeah."

Who's supposed to talk now, me or Chloe? I forgot who talked last. I guess it's my turn: "So, listen, I wanted to know if you want to hang out sometime this week, you know? I can get you more frozen yogurt or—"

"Party."

"What?"

"There's a party at Jason Finderman's house because his parents got busted for money laundering, so they're in, ah, Barbados?"

"Uh-huh."

"So it's going to be this Saturday and he has a pool and the whole deal."

"Wow. Is it like, bring your own liquor or whatever?"

"I don't really care . . . I'm rolling. You rolling?"

Very luckily, I know what that means. Thank you, squip. "Hold on a second, Chloe."

I turn the squip on and ask: Can we roll? You know, do ecstasy?

I DO NOT RECOMMEND IT. I HAVE TO BE OFF FOR IT. IF YOU DO IT, YOU MIGHT HOOK UP WITH CHLOE, BUT YOU MIGHT JUST—

"Okay, sure, I'll do it," I say back to the phone.

"Really? You will? With me? Aww, Jeremy, you're so sweet."

"Heh, yeah, rockin', you know."

"Rockin'?"

ROCKIN'?

"I was talking to the TV."

Chloe laughs. "So these are twenty-five dollar rolls. Can you give me the money at school?"

$25? WE'RE GOING TO HAVE TO GET SOME MONEY—

"Sure, I'll give it to you," I say quickly.

"And here's the important question . . . do you have a *car*, Jeremy?"

"Yeah, oh sure. I'll definitely have one for this party, absolutely."

WE'RE GOING TO HAVE TO STEAL ONE FROM YOUR PARENTS, OR BRING MICHAEL.

I'll bring Michael anyway. We'll handle it.

"Okay, great, so does that mean you can, like, *drive me home* after the party?"

"Sure!"

"It's gonna take a while for the rolls to wear off, but I have to be home by dawn-break, y'know?"

"That shouldn't be a problem."

"So we'll meet in school and you'll give me the money, okay?"

"Great."

"See you, Jeremy!" And she hangs up. Damn, that girl knows how to take charge. Now all I need to do is get money and a car.

Your Mom's purse is by the dining room table. She won't miss $25.

That's the easy part. We're going to want Mom's ride too, right? (Mom has a decent ride, a Nissan Maxima. Dad's is not so good.)

Yes. Get ready for a lesson, Jeremy. Driving's easy. Like the video games.

I'm up for it.

thirty-
one

I get Chloe her money in school, where everyone is talking about Jason Finderman's party. It's weird, now; it's like I automatically know what's going on, like I don't have to sit forward and analyze it or agonize over it; it just comes to me. I pass people in the hall—not lots of people, just a few important ones like Rich and Brooke—and they fill me in on everything that's happening: Anne did this; Jenna did this; this party is this weekend; this guy got in this car accident; this kid has herpes. And while I'm talking to them, other people pass me by, people like Michael Mell—people at his status level—and they look at me the same way they look at Rich and Brooke. As a superior.

Simple things, that's what the squip is fixing. Clothes are first. You need certain clothes and the best way to decide which ones is to have a computer do it for you. To do fashion any other way would just take too much time—I don't know how squipless people do it.

Then, it's really good to get to school early. You chill out on the steps a little, see who's coming in, see who's in a rush and who's not, see if anyone wants to smoke or drink or have a cigarette before school—although they're all dummy cigarettes to me. (The squip says cigarette smoke impairs its analytical reasoning powers.) You don't get hit with nerd penalty points for being there early.

Also, you never rush anywhere. If you run to class, you're showing the world that class is more important to you than you. So you walk, but you don't slink. You walk purposefully, with your chest out, thinking in grunts so that you maintain that base-level competitiveness with other men. You view high school as a death-match jungle arena, because that's what it is.

If you see a girl and she makes any kind of eye contact with you, you *have* to smile at her. The squip explained that to me this way: OKAY, JEREMY, HOW DO YOU KNOW IF A GIRL LIKES YOU?

Um . . .

LET ME GIVE YOU A CLUE. WHAT IS THE SENSORY PERCEPT THAT HUMAN BEINGS EMPLOY MOST TO ENCODE THEIR SURROUNDINGS?

I'm sorry?

HOW DO PEOPLE VIEW THE WORLD?

Uh, the news?

EYES, JEREMY. THE EYES. DIDN'T YOU EVER HEAR THAT EXPRESSION, "THE EYES HAVE IT"?

No.

WELL THEY DO.

What do they have?

IT, JEREMY. THE EYES TELL YOU WHICH GIRLS LIKE YOU.

Okay, so I have to look at girls?

NO, YOU HAVE TO SEE WHICH GIRLS LOOK AT YOU.

Ah. None of them do.

SURE THEY DO. YOU JUST DON'T NOTICE. OR IF YOU DO CATCH ONE LOOKING, YOU LOOK DOWN AND DON'T DO ANYTHING ABOUT IT AND YOUR FAILURE TO ACT PAINS YOU SO MUCH THAT YOU FORGET ABOUT IT IN FIVE MINUTES.

That sounds right.

SO FROM NOW ON, I WANT YOU TO CHECK TO SEE IF ANY GIRLS LOOK AT YOU. AND IF ONE DOES, YOU HAVE TO SMILE AT HER.

That's hard.

OF COURSE IT'S HARD! WHAT, YOU THINK THIS STUFF IS EASY? WHEN YOU BECOME SEXUALLY AROUSED, YOUR DICK GETS HARD TOO, DOESN'T IT?

Theoretically.

NOT THEORETICALLY. I'M THERE WHEN IT HAPPENS. SO THE POINT IS SOME THINGS ARE HARD IN THIS WORLD, JEREMY. GOOD THINGS.

Right. So if—

YOU MUST LOOK AT ALL THE GIRLS WHO PASS YOUR WAY. DON'T STARE AT THEM, JUST SCAN THEM VERY CAREFULLY, SUBTLY, TO SEE IF THEY ARE EYEING YOU. AND IF THEY ARE, SMILE AT THEM IMMEDIATELY, AS IF YOU CAN'T HELP IT, THEY'RE JUST SO CUTE. THAT'S HOW YOU DISTINGUISH YOURSELF IN THIS WORLD: INSTEAD OF BEING THE GUY WHO LEERS AT THEM, YOU'LL BE THE GUY WHO SMILES AT THEM. IT'S GOING TO TAKE A LOT OF WORK BECAUSE SMILING USES THIRTY-SEVEN MUSCLES, BUT I'LL BOOST THOSE MUSCLES FOR YOU.

Okay.

IF YOU DON'T, YOU'RE NEVER GOING TO GET LAID. IT'S THE FIRST STEP.

And so I smile. At first I end up with these crooked, premature smiles that look like I have spinach stuck in my teeth and I'm trying to roll it out with my lips. But I get better with practice, to the point where I can bend over at the water fountain, see which girls are looking at me (since I'm at their level) and smile with water sloshing off my teeth, like an Oral-B ad.

Oh, yeah, I have an Oral-B electric toothbrush now, one of many consumer adjustments. I started buying Crest Whitening Strips too, which I wear in my teeth while I do push-ups in front of the TV. They work wonders. I also got Tegrin antidandruff shampoo, the strongest you can buy without a prescription. It's dark green and smells like tar, but even it doesn't cure my dandruff until the squip tells me to use my nails in the shower and gouge at my scalp to get the Tegrin to my guilty skin cells. I spend a lot more time in the bathroom now.

In this enviable state—cleaned up, decked out, well dressed, flake-free, and at once socially hyperconscious and totally at ease—I give Chloe $25 for my roll. It's a particularly fine day because at the start, in math, we solved the attendance problem.

"Caniglia," Mr. Gretch said.

"Here."

"Duvoknovich."

"Here."

"Goranski."

"Here."

"Heere?"

"Yo."

It was so simple. Mr. Gretch didn't mind and everyone in the class sort of shuffled around to look at me, saying "Yo" from the back. I smiled at them. I don't know how I didn't think of it before. IT'S NOT YOUR NATURE, the squip said.

About two minutes after that, Jenna went into her thing about "Elizabeth let four guys do her on the bus" and I had the balls to say what I've always wanted to say, deadpan: "Shut up, Jenna. We know

'Elizabeth' is like your Spider-Slut alterego or something."

And Anne laughed and laughed and Mark Jackson laughed and Mr. Gretch didn't hear and Jenna, at least for a few seconds, really did shut up.

thirty-two

"So, Michael, you want to go to a party on Saturday?"
I ask him out of the blue. I don't know how much
"blue" can be established in ten days, but it seems
like a lot. Michael's playing handball by himself
against the mural outside school with his headphones on, not listening to anything.

"Hey, Jeremy," he says.

WHY ARE YOU STILL DEALING WITH THIS GUY?

Hold on. "Yeah, so you want to go to this party?" I
assume. I mean I just assume. He could answer.

"No." He holds his ball, looks at me. "I got a question for you, man. You remember medieval Legos?"

"Sure."

"Remember how we lost the original trees so we
had to use palm trees outside the castles even though
it was supposed to be a deciduous European forest?"

"Yeah."

"Remember that *anachronism*?"

"Yes."

"Oh. Just checking. I thought you were maybe doing a revisionist thing with your nerd—"

"C'mon, man—"

"Now that you're a swinger and all."

WE ARE SWINGERS. HE'S RIGHT!

I smile. "It's not like that. Really. I want you to come to this party."

"F_c_ you, Jeremy. You still haven't apologized for ditching me at the mall."

"Yes I did!" I say. "And if I didn't, I'm apologizing now. I apologize for not apologizing. This whole party is an apology."

"You don't want me at any party. You want me to *drive* you to that party."

"No, man! I'm going myself."

"How?"

"I'm gonna try some drivin' skillz." I imagine a *Z*.

"Jeremy . . ." Michael's voice gets quiet. "If you're gonna be stupid, I'll take you in my car. Don't get killed."

I look at Michael's ride, parked in the parking lot like a used condom. Not used properly. I don't want anyone seeing me in that thing.

CORRECT.

"C'mon man, I can drive. I want to drive myself."

"No you can't, Jeremy! You've never done it in your life!"

"So how hard can it be, man? C'mon, man."

Michael holds the handball close to his chest. "If you're going to do something that *stupid*," he says, "then I'll go with you, just to make sure you don't die or anything."

DON'T BRING HIM.

Nope, I'm bringing him. I want him along on this one. I've wanted him along the whole time, but now I finally have the clout to bring him.

STRONG PARAMETER MISMATCH.

Well, it doesn't matter. Didn't you say I could include him in my new circle once I made it?

STRONG PARAMETER MISMATCH.

Shutdown.

"Uh, I assume that's a 'yes'?" Michael says.

"Yeah, you're coming." I reach out to slap his hand; he responds the way we used to slap— flat-handed—so I show him the new way, the curvy way the squip showed me.

thirty-three

THAT LOOKS GREAT! the squip exclaims. TOTALLY EFFECTIVE!

I look in the mirror at my naked body. It's more buff than I ever imagined, two weeks in, and totally hairless—the squip made me use candle wax to get out the five or so hairs that it found near my pecs. Unfortunately I can't focus on anything other than the two straight marks that line my thighs, below my abdomen. The squip convinced me to paint these, a *V* around my crotch, outlining those "sartorius" muscles that didn't develop so well in my exercise program. I did them with a Sharpie; they're smooth and uniform, as if I were an action figure with bendable legs. It's stupid.

NO, IT'S NOT. YOU RESEMBLE ASHTON KUTCHER. REMEMBER, ASHTON KUTCHER BEST REPRESENTS THE SEXUALITY THAT ENTHRALLS PRESENT-DAY FEMALES.

Right. Boyish yet . . . what?

BOYISH YET CASUALLY SUPERHUMAN. YOU READY TO GO?

I put my party clothes on and start down the stairs. It's nine o'clock, Saturday night; Mom is off somewhere with her legal briefs and Dad is watching football in the kitchen.

"Okay, so I'm out," I tell him as I pass his setup: my Dad, a chair, a beer, peanut butter, Oreo cookies, and the TV arranged for maximum comfort, like a science experiment.

"Huh," Dad says. "Well, have a good time and all." He breaks his concentration to actually look at me while he dips an Oreo into the peanut butter. It's a Peanut Butter Oreo anyway. "Seriously, have a *great* time. I remember my first real party."

"Heh, yeah," I look down. PERFECT. BE INNOCENT. "Michael's going to be here any minute so I'm gonna go on the porch and wait for him."

"Huh."

I stride out of my house and immediately crouch, ninja-style. GREAT. TO THE DRIVEWAY. I crab walk down the porch, clutching the side of the house, careful not to trip over the coiled hose. I'm at the edge of the kitchen window; Mom's car is in front of me, sleek and inviting, lit by the one fake gas porch light and the streetlamps out beyond the lawn. I'm going to replace it with Michael's car once he gets here so Dad'll be less likely to notice a car missing if he decides to pee outside, which he does sometimes after football.

CALL NOW.

I pick up my cell phone, phone home. I can hear Dad moving from the kitchen to the living room, grumbling. Just before he would pick up—three and a half rings—I hit the beeper on the keychain I took from his pants while he was having private time with Mom (he always leaves his pants in the hall). *Beep boop beep*, the car says.

HANG UP.

I click the *End* button just as I hear Dad say "Hello?" He's in the living room, annoyed, deciding whether or not to dial *69. Since I know he's away from the kitchen window, I scamper by to the car door, open it up and sit in the driver's seat. Awesome.

AWESOME. NOW THE EMERGENCY BRAKE.

It smells like Mom in the car. I clutch the brake between the two front seats with my fist, press it in and set it on the floor. Mom's car—my car, whatever—starts rolling down the driveway; I freak and slam the brakes. The wheels make a little skidding noise.

JEREMY. DON'T LOSE IT NOW. EASE BACK ONTO THE ROAD. EVERYTHING'S FINE.

I lift my foot off the brake, letting the car ooze comfortably back down a dozen more feet. TURN, TURN. I do as I'm told. Amazingly—just like in *Test*

Drive—the car turns sweetly backward onto my street, Rampart Road, and I execute what looks like a pretty competent parking job next to Ms. Daniels's house. A BORN DRIVER. I KNEW YOU COULD DO IT.

I look at the driveway. I ran over some grass but, all in all, it was an excellent gambit. Now I just have to wait for Michael to show up. I turn on the radio, twisting the keys in the steering column toward me, the "safe" way, the way I was taught to, so I don't start the engine. I power down the driver's side window and look out at airplanes in the sky. And satellites. The squip tells me that most of the stars you see are actually satellites.

THAT ONE'S CLASSIFIED. GREEK MILITARY.

The Greeks have a satellite?

SURE. THAT ONE'S FOR AT&T. SO'S THAT ONE. THAT'S JAPANESE.

What about that one?

THAT'S SIRIUS. A REAL STAR.

After five minutes (each minute is cold, but also sharp), Michael's s__t car rolls up to my house. He's expecting me on the porch, not out here, so I get out and walk to his window, tap on it and wave at him.

"Put your car in my driveway."

"Okay," he grins. He's having fun.

I call home again as Michael pulls into the driveway, as a distraction. A very perturbed Dad answers.

"Yeah."

"Yeah, Dad, Michael came and picked me up, so I'm on my way to this party, okay?"

"Fine, son. Have your friends been prank calling here?"

"No."

"If they do, I'm serious, I'll go balliztic on their asses."

"'Balliztic?'"

"Yeah, like the rappers do? You know, *Niggaz Go Balliztic*? That album?"

"Um, okay, Dad. See ya."

I end the call as Michael walks up to me on Rampart Road, silent. We traipse on the glittering asphalt to Mom's car.

"Isn't your Dad going to notice the difference between this car and mine?" Michael says.

"Think about it. It'll be night and he'll really need to come up to it and look closely, plus he'll be so happy or devastated, depending on how his game turns out . . . I don't think we have anything to worry about."

THAT'S BECAUSE I CALCULATED IT FOR YOU, STUPID.

I know. Thanks.

Michael and I get in my Mom's car. I jam the key in the steering column and turn it away from me this time, the way I was instructed *never* to do. The engine comes to life. My body tingles like I'm on

Internet chat, like I'm talking with Christine, like I'm doing everything all at once. Driving is going to rock.

REMEMBER: BOTH HANDS ON THE WHEEL AT TEN AND TWO. USE ONLY ONE FOOT TO DRIVE. IF YOU USE BOTH FEET, YOU'RE LIABLE TO PUT A FOOT ON THE BRAKE AND ACCELERATOR AT THE SAME TIME, AND YOU DON'T WANT THAT. SHIFT INTO "D" AND KEEP IN MIND THAT THE WHEEL IS MUCH MORE SENSITIVE THAN IT IS IN VIDEO GAMES. YOU SHOULD NEVER HAVE TO TURN THEATRICALLY, LIKE JAMES BOND.

I do as I'm told. With the squip in my head, I drive steadily and carefully, anticipating other cars, the behavior patterns of red lights, unseen bumps, and objects in the mirrors. The squip says it can sense these things through quantum entanglement, but I'm beginning to think it's just magic.

"Damn, you're a good driver," Michael says. "You gotta get your license and ferry me around more often."

I smile. Michael overdressed, wearing a blue button-down shirt and khaki cargo pants instead of anything remotely cool. (I'm in a designer tee, used jeans, and a baseball cap at a jaunty angle.) But I think I'll be able to get him with a girl at this party, if he keeps his mouth shut.

"Here we go."

"Already? It was like two minutes away!"

"Yeah, but you still need to come in a *car*."

The street is clogged with parked vehicles. It's easy to tell where the action is: one house has a T-shirt and bra out on the front lawn, all the lights except one on inside, and what looks like a stream of urine emanating from a third-story window.

"Wow, supercool," Michael grins as we stop.

LAST CHANCE TO LEAVE HIM IN THE CAR.

No. He's my friend.

We get out and stride across the lawn like gangsters. Or at least, *I'm* a gangster (gangsta, even?— maybe not yet); Michael is still learning, but some of me is rubbing off on him. How could it not? He's starting to get the walk, the posture. At the door is some guy I've never seen before, with freckles. I hate freckles.

"Hi, I'm Jason's brother . . ." He shakes hands prissily. "Do you know who Jason is?"

"Yeah, he's the guy throwing the party," I spit.

"Ri-ight, well, there are already a lot of people here, so he sent me out here to tell everybody who comes that—"

TELL THIS GUY TO KISS YOUR STEAMING A_ _ _O_ _ .

"Kiss my—"

"Jeremy!" Chloe screams from one story up, leaning out a window. "You're here!"

"Yeah, hey," I look up, stretching my Adam's apple.

"Carl, let him in, and his friend too," she tells the door guy. "Don't be a complete dick to everyone, just stupid people!"

"O-o-okay," Carl says, stepping aside to let us into the party. Inside it's kids everywhere, bright and noisy, crouched in corners and on steps and on couches and rubbing up against one another in crevices. There must be sixty of them in here, but I only get a vague impression because immediately Chloe is bounding down the stairs at me, leaping over the people like gargoyles, flinging her arms around my neck. *"Hi!"*

She expertly shoves a pill in my mouth. Hey, where did Michael go? Did he leave to find beer?

"I said *hi-i-i!*" Chloe grins. She taps a bottle of water against the side of my head. "Keep that, it's your magic water!"

"Okay." The music in the party is deafening. It's like a different dimension.

"So what are you waiting for? Take your pill, before it dissolves!" Chloe freaks. I swig the water and swallow obediently. "Is that like, *the* pill?" I ask.

"Dur!" Chloe sticks her tongue out at me.

I SUGGEST YOU TURN ME OFF NOW, JEREMY. YOU DON'T WANT ME ON WHILE YOU'RE ROLLING. AS WE DISCUSSED.

Right. Shutdown.

thirty-four

There's unbelievable anticipation in my nervous system as I move through the house, led by Chloe's small ring finger. I know that at some point my brain is going to explode with pleasure or insanity or . . . y'know, *something*, and waiting for it is almost as crazy as whatever it's going to be. I'm ready, though. I've had a voice in my head for weeks. What could there be inside me that's more intense than the squip?

Chloe wears jeans with sequins and a shirt with intentional holes in it. She maneuvers past kids grinding to hip-hop, kids smoking weed on what looks like inflatable plastic furniture, past Rich and whoever's attached to his belly button this week (he smiles at me, making a clicking noise), and Jenna Rolan and that kid Eric with the one eyebrow, and all the faces that I see now instead of just admire. (Unfortunately, no Michael. Where did he go?) Jesus, even Christine is here! She's in one of the living rooms (but they all look like living rooms when they have enough people in them) by herself! No Jake in sight! This is my chance!

"Chloe, I've got to—" I tug at her arm, dab my chin toward Christine. At the same time, since this is going to be an important conversation, I turn the squip on.

WHAT ARE YOU DOING? LEAVE CHRISTINE ALONE. CHLOE IS GOING TO LEAD YOU TO A ROOM FOR ECSTASY-LADEN SEXUAL SHENAGIANS! REMEMBER, CHRISTINE WILL COME LATER—

But she's available now!

"You really live in your own little world, don't you?" Chloe asks, standing next to me, watching me stare at Christine, who hasn't noticed yet.

"No, I just—"

"Come!" Chloe grabs my shirt. "I *like* you." She adjusts my baseball cap. "You can go back to your world later. Be in mine for a while."

I look at Chloe. She really *is* cute, this time with a pastel candy bracelet around her neck. This is not a problem I ever thought I'd have.

THAT'S RIGHT, AND YOU DON'T HAVE ONE NOW. GO WITH THE GIRL WHO'S TOUCHING YOU.

I clasp Chloe's hand and let her lead me out of the room, through the house, to a thin door that looks like it goes to a closet, but actually opens into a laundry center, with a washer and two small dryers and a mattress on the floor and some jalapeño-shaped Christmas lights on the pipes. Chloe pushes me in. She shuts the door very quickly, locking it; I have this sudden flash that she's hiding from someone, that just as I'm trying to talk to Christine, she's trying *not* to talk to somebody, but then she's kissing me and taking my hat off and it's a lot nicer than with Brooke and we're leaning back and I'm shutting the squip off for good because her face is shimmering in front of mine.

The music comes through the walls slow and distorted; I only hear the bass rumble. It's one of those techno songs where the beat doubles and redoubles and redoubles again every two seconds until it's a superfast hummingbird blur and then it stops and there's a wooshing electronic voice that goes, *"Ex-stasy."* And then the beat starts again. Chloe and I fall like slow trees to the mattress, tongues working like philosopher starfish. I can't even pinpoint the moment when we started kissing; I just know we are. Both of us have our eyes open but we don't care.

"Omigosh," Chloe pulls away, wiping my spit from her lips. "It's hitting you." She looks deeply at me. "Your eyes are doing the pupil-shake!" She seems so happy. "Here, have more of your magic water!" She takes it out of my pocket, where I put it without realizing.

"But . . ." I push the water away; it rolls down the

floor. Chloe is looking so good right now and so sexy and so much like she was born for me, for this moment, that I have to sit up and grab her and lean her in my lap and start playing with her breasts through her shirt with the holes, just like the squip told me to do before with Brooke. (Holes make it easy.) I'm very warm (I'm sweating) and I'm leaning forward in a way I can't help and chewing on Chloe's candy necklace and thinking about sex in its most basic, pure, mechanical form, like what I see in the little movies on the Internet, close up. And I start talking: "Oh man, Chloe, I want to _ _ _ _ you so bad, right? I want to pull on your _ _ _ _les, right? And then I want to _ _ _ _ on your _ _ _ _, right? Right? And then I can _ _ _ _ _ _ _ _ and _ _ _, right? _ _ _ _ _ _ _?" My words seem to have rhythm, something primal and stuttered to the music, or something.

"Mmm," Chloe mmms from my lap. I keep going. I'm on a dirty-talking roll, like the kind I get into on Internet chat. The words flow: "And then I'm gonna b_ _ _ on your _ _ _ _ and _ _ _ _ your shoulders and _ _ _ your knee, right? And then I'm gonna _ _ _ _ _ _ _ _ your tail—"

"Jeremy! I don't have a tail!" Chloe laughs.

"Yeah, but I really wish you did, right? Like I would paste a tail right on you. Like a little monkey tail. I had dreams about you and in them, you always had a tail, you know?"

"Jeremy." Chloe gets up, pushes me down on the mattress. "You're so weird." She's perched over me now, hands to either side of my shoulders and knees to either side of my waist.

"Are you 'straddling' me?" I ask, wide-eyed. "Is this called 'straddling?'"

Sweat rolls into my eye. Chloe's impossible gorgeous elfin face shudders. "Have you ever rolled before?"

I shake my head extravagantly. "I've never done *anything* before," I say. "My sq—, uh, my special friend won't let me." Phew.

"You *are* weird . . . my little rolling virgin," Chloe says, coming in to kiss more. She lets me take off her shirt, but her bra, which I couldn't handle in a normal mind state, is out of the question. (It seems to have holes in it too—how did she put holes in the bra?) She rears up, unleashes it herself, and I aim right for them (they're so beautiful, bigger than Brooke's) in a state of deathless shock—

"Wait, Jeremy, let me show you something," Chloe says, and she's about to show me this something, whatever it is (it must be *amazing*), when there's a horrible crash as the tiny window above the washing machine shatters and a huge fist emerges, bloody.

"Chloe!"

"Omigod!" Chloe grabs her shirt, which she knew

was at the foot of the mattress, and clutches it over her breasts.

"You _ _ _k _ _ slut!" the fist says, and I see that it's not bloody; it's tattooed in this weird way that makes it look like ink is spilling out between each knuckle. "You *whore!*"

Now an eye appears at the window, like a whale eye, except I realize that it's not a whale, that some belligerent *person* has punched through from outside and that we're below ground level and he's up on the lawn. And as I'm putting this together, not really acknowledging my own role in the situation, the eye moves in the window and is replaced by a mouth, and the mouth says: "Jeremy Heere. I am going to knock your teeth down your throat."

"Watch out, Jeremy; it's my boyfriend!" Chloe yells, dressing as quickly as she undressed. She unlatches the door and is suddenly gone, blowing me a kiss like this is a French movie and I'm the unlikely hero. I'm alone in the laundry room. The eye and the mouth are gone. Where is he? *Who* is he? I grab my magic water and drink it all. Oh God, the whole room is shaking . . . undulating . . . vacillating. It's so *hot*. Who is Chloe's boyfriend? I have to have kept track of him from earlier in the year. It's some jock guy. I thought they broke up. His name is . . .

The squip! How could I forget? Startup.

TU ESTÁS EN UN SITUACIÓN MUY PELIGROSO.

What the—?

Tu estás en el peligro grave, Jeremy. ¡Salga del cuarto!

Spanish?

Sí, español, estúpido. Éste es qué sucede cuando intento comunicarme mientras que usted está en ecstasy.

But I suck at Spanish! All I know are the colors— ¡Rojo!

Red!

¡Alarma roja!

Something red?

¡Alarma roja, Jeremy! ¡Alarma roja!

Red alarm?

¡Alarma roja!

Red *alert*! Right, this guy's coming to beat my ass. I gotta get out of here. I drop everything, which is nothing, and run from the laundry room.

"Yo," the jock says. He's in the hall, at the bottom of the stairs. I don't remember coming down any stairs to get in here, but I do remember this guy's name finally; it's one of the toughest names in school to forget: Brock.

"I'm gonna _ u _ _ _ _ _ kill you," Brock says.

¡Pato y jab, Jeremy! ¡Golpéelo con el pie en las bolas!

Shutdown. Jesus, I don't have time for this.

Brock runs toward me with alarming speed for

someone so big. Like those what's-their-faces, croco-diles. But I'm better evolved than a crocodile. I turn and sprint down the hall. There's a door up ahead, but it looks like a tricky double door, like one wood door that opens toward me and behind that, a screen door that opens away, and behind that, concrete stairs leading up to the lawn. As long as I can get myself out those doors and into the cold air, I'll be okay. At least I won't be so hot. I don't want to get beat up when it's so hot.

"*Ugggghh,*" Brock says as he reaches for me while I duck, shoot my hand up, twist the doorknob and pull it toward me. "*Ngaaa!*" Brock hits his face on the side of the door! Awesome! Just like I planned! I'm crouched between the door and the wall, like we were playing hide-and-go-seek and this was the only spot available at the last second. Brock is stumbling around, dazed, holding his nose.

I kick open the screen door and run into the night air, vaulting up the concrete stairs three at a time to the lawn. Brock has recovered and is after me. Out on the grass, kids are setting off lame fire-related works and making out. I almost step on Ryu's head as I screech through the human traffic and back around to the front of the house, the start of the party. What's-his-name, Carl, the door guard, starts to say something at me, but I hold out my arm and clip him as I run headlong into his place. F _ _ _ everybody! Ecstasy is not a loving drug!

Where is Brock, huh? Was it that easy? I slink carefully through the partygoers and their limbs, sure I've lost him. I'm too fast. I'm too good and I'm too cool and you can't stop me. Never. I'm Jeremy Heere. But just to be safe I decide to get to the second floor and hide in whatever bedroom I can find. So I wind up the stairs, make a big left turn at the top and jiggle the first doorknob I come across. I push it open hard.

It's not a bedroom; it's a bathroom. The door was jammed shut with a female shoe, but that wasn't enough. I stomp inside and Stephanie the Hot Girl is there, black hair making quite a contrast with the toilet, retching in the bowl.

thirty-five

"What the _ _ _ _?" Stephanie screeches at me, whirling around with stringy spit on her chin. "What are you doing here? Who *are* you?! Get out!"

"I'm in trouble, right? I have to hide," I explain quickly, putting my finger to my lips. I take one long look at her: she's drunk and teary-eyed and streaked with barf, but she's still one of the top three girls in school. She turns back to the toilet; I crawl under the bathroom sink and stuff myself next to the cold, curved pipe, which sweats clean-smelling water droplets. I shut the cabinet door with a clawed finger. I hear the bathroom door open.

"What the _ _ _ _?" Stephanie repeats.

"Wuh?" Brock's voice answers. "Oh, sorry, I'm just looking for somebody—"

"Well, I'm just *drunk*, okay? Would you leave?!"

The door closes. After a minute or so in the black under the sink (I stay very quiet) an irregular drip starts to drive me crazy. Not that it's dripping on me; I can just hear it and it's really gross, human-sounding. After a while I realize it's Stephanie letting excess, watery, pre-vomity spit trickle out of her mouth and into the toilet.

"Tough night, huh?" I put the words together with effort, making them loud enough for her to hear.

"Yeah."

"That kid who came in, he wants to kill me. So thanks for helping out."

"I don't know if I meant to help out," Stephanie giggles (of all things). "I mean, I just totally forgot you were under there—*bwaaaaark*!"

"Jeez, are you okay?"

"Never."

"That's, um, too bad." I hear her get up; she takes three steps across the bathroom floor and sends a soft rush of water down the pipe at me as she washes her hands. Her palms squeak against each other. "I'm rolling," I venture from my inferior, interior position.

"*Really?*" Stephanie opens the cabinet door, her pretty white face blocking the light. "Do you have more?"

"Nope," I shake my head.

"Well, screw *you*, then." She closes the door, a grin in her voice. "You're no use."

"Heh, yeah. Never. Not to anybody." I'm back in darkness. "Do you have gum?"

"Sure." The cabinet door opens a crack, hesitantly, as if Stephanie were using her foot. A stick of gum is ushered in at me. I take it with my teeth.

"Thanks," I say, chewing in the dark. "I figured since you were throwing up you'd have gum."

"I wasn't throwing up."

"What were you doing, then? Clearing your sinuses?" I chew.

"I was having *dry heaves*," Stephanie explains. "I threw up *before*."

"Why?"

"Well, I cut myself," Stephanie says. "I cut myself and the *guilt* makes me throw up."

"That's too bad," I say. "Can you open this door and let me hold your leg?"

"What?"

"Just your leg. Anything warm. Anything but this pipe."

With a sigh, the cabinet door opens. Bathroom light makes me keep my head low as I crawl out from under the sink and grip Stephanie's left leg. Then I look up at her. She looks interested in me only as an anthropological specimen. She wears a black Goth semidress that's less like human clothing and more like one of those choker vines that destroys its host tree and leaves its dead shell clinging to thin air. Her neck is encircled by a collar with chrome studs.

"You're that guy Chloe likes!" she says above me,

a stud sticking out parallel to her nose, her breasts giant mountains. "Jeremy!"

"Yes," I squeeze.

"Wow, you're rolling hard." Stephanie bends down and cups my chin. "Chloe was right; you're not that cute. You're supposed to be really cool, though."

"Yeah?"

"Yeah. You're supposed to be, like, you kinda keep to yourself and don't say much, but you're really good at something, or something."

"I'm good at everything!" I smile. I let go of the leg, stand up, pull my shirt to my chin and show off my pecs. "I have a toned body. See?"

"What are those?" Stephanie points at the tops of my fake sartorius muscles.

"Uh, birthmarks."

"Er, excuse me?" says someone outside the bathroom.

"*Shhh*," Stephanie and I both *shhh*. "I have a cute butt!" I say, bending over the sink to show her. "I know about TV. I like the same things that you like! I have no dandruff—"

"You're really funny," Stephanie smiles, putting her hand on my back. "Do you want to see my extragorgeous new tattoo?"

"Sure."

She slowly pulls up the bottom of her dress, revealing the leg that I held a second ago. "See, it's not a tattoo in the modern sense," she explains. "The Polynesians used tattoo in very basic, geometric-type patterns. Like lines and stuff?"

Now her skirt is up to her knee. She twists; I see the scabbed-over cut marks that divide her calf into very precise half-centimeters. They stretch like railroad tracks all the way from her ankle up to where her rumpled dress ends—I bet they go up farther than that. They're neat, razorlike, laserlike, potent, shallow, and thin.

"Ugg . . ."

"Aren't they pretty? That's why I do them. They're so pretty; they're like the only beauty in my world." She knocks her knees together as if she's a little girl incredibly pleased with herself.

"Oh man," I say, backing away. I choke out one word, and it's not the word I mean to say: "—weird."

"I know," Stephanie says, opening her eyes wide. "I'm *tragically* weird." She swishes out of the bathroom. "Bye, Jeremy!" She leaves me by the sink, holding on to nothing. Two drunk kids pile in after her and do a double-decker vomit attack on the toilet. They don't notice me.

thirty-six

"Michael!"

I stumble down the hall on the second floor, sucking in my frame to squeeze by people leaning against walls, making out with each other and holding each other's hair. This really sucks. I want to lie down somewhere and hold a pillow or a body or something, but there are no pillows and no bodies and no beds and no rooms and no friends! All my friends are downstairs; up here it's a lot of loser kids who didn't want to be friends with me before the squip and who I don't need now. It's mostly the losers who are hooking up. Or playing video games.

"Michael!"

Who else am I supposed to ask for? Christine would be good to see but she's probably not alone in some room anymore—she's probably been snapped up by Jake Dillinger.

"Yo, Jeremy!"

Brock! No, wait, it's Rich, calling from the stairs. I walk a few paces back and look down at him. He's halfway between the first and second floor, his sweaty blond hair in his eyes. The red streak has come around to the front.

"What?"

"You _ _ _ _ _d up or something?" he asks. Loud.

"Well, kind of—"

"Then come downstairs! You gotta see this!" Rich doesn't bother going up the rest of the way; he just turns and bumps down, banking from banister to banister. I follow more slowly. At the bottom of the steps, in the main living room, Rich makes a right turn. We skirt the couches and go down a green hall. At the end of the hall is a door. The door could be open or it could be closed; I can't tell because it's teeming with teenage male life. Guys are crammed around it so tightly that some of them have piled on top of each other, in a sort of cheerleading pyramid, to see inside. (So the door must be open.) The guys are murmuring to one another, concentrating. They're surprisingly quiet.

"It's the only way," Rich says. "You gotta see this. Duck down." He crawls on his belly toward the door and I follow, shimmying up to the bottom of the pyramid. I can just barely peek through someone's calves into the room. There's thick carpeting. A pair of sneakers stand by what looks like a bed.

"What is it?"

"Man, c'mon, are you stupid or what? Jake Dillinger has Katrina in there and we're watching."

"Oh, wow—Jake?" I mumble. "Those are Jake's feet?"

"Yeah."

"Wow." I stare at the cool feet. "Hey, where does that leave Christine?"

"Shut up and watch!"

Jake's feet aren't moving much and Katrina's feet aren't visible at all—they must be spread out and up. If I look up to try and see more, all I get is a little bit of the ceiling and the crotches, shrouded in pants, of the boys above me. I do *hear* lots, though: mostly Jake grunting, which sounds like the grunting he does with his football buddies, and little whimpery noises from Katrina, like the ones Brooke made when I kissed her, the ones that mean "keep going," and then the occasionally responsive "Whoa" from Jake. There's also the constant murmur of the boys, making sure that everybody shuts up so Katrina doesn't hear them and they can all make their witty comments. And there's the underpinning bass rumble of rap.

It's sad that I get turned on by this. It's very similar to the sex I enjoy on my own—voyeur sex, cybersex, looking at movies and pictures, seeing other people and wondering what it would be like if they were me. I feel that glow in my crotch and I smile and I'm ashamed.

"This sucks," Rich says next to me, like a snake. "You could see everything before. I guess we're going to have to depend on Carlton."

"Carlton Hafer-Mules?"

"Yeah."

"Dyed-his-*neck*-hair-Carlton? Is he up there?" I nod at the guys above me.

"Yeah." Rich seems to think that's the most obvious thing in the world. "He has a great digital camera. He puts up pictures of the Hot Girls all the time. Lots of Stephanie and Chloe, but mostly Katrina."

"You're kidding."

"Course not. Try KatrinaStephanieChloe.com."

"Jeez . . . You know I saw Stephanie and Chloe earlier tonight?"

"Yeah, man! I heard you went to the basement with Chloe! What happened?"

"Nothing. Nothing good."

"Jeremy, what's wrong with you? Even with a squip you can't get laid? What—"

"Oh, man . . ." Jake mumbles from his room of sex. Then, unbelievably, there's some kind of farting noise. The whole libido pyramid above me shudders with laughter.

"Whoa!"

"I didn't even know that could happen. . . ."

"Get it on tape! Did someone get it on tape?"

"Guys, don't let me fall!"

My whole leg goes dead as someone teeters off the mountain and lands on my calf.

"Aggh," I hear a moan behind me. "My spine . . ."

I wriggle backward and turn over. My leg hurts like it got pegged with a girder, but the other guy landed on his back; you can really mess yourself up landing on your back. "Are you all right?" I ask. He's rolled off me and is sitting by the wall.

"Yeah, of course," he shrugs. It's Eric, the guy with the one eyebrow.

"Eric."

"Yeah, hey, Jeremy, right? Thanks for breaking my fall. I heard you stopped doing those sheet things." Eric scrambles back up the pile to watch more of Katrina and Jake. Screw him. Screw this.

"Where are you going?" Rich asks from the floor as I limp down the hall to the living room. I say nothing. When I get to the room, one make-out couple has graciously moved from a couch to the floor so I have a place to hibernate. I get on the couch and remove the cushions and hold one of them to my chest and roll into the crook of the furniture and try to control myself as the world shimmers around me with a pleasure that's so empty. Right? I think about Christine; she must be sad that the guy she's dating is banging some other girl down the hall and getting photographed for a Web site.

Stupid and alone and on drugs, I activate the squip.

IDIOTA, IDIOTA, IDIOTA. TODO LO QUE USTED ES BUENO PARA ES SEXO DEL INTERNET.

All I'm good for is sex on the Internet. Shutdown.

thirty-seven

"Jeremy, do you want some water?"

"Yes please," I say, not knowing who I'm saying yes to, only that it's a girl. And that I said please (like I'm supposed to). I turn around like a dolphin. My eyes have been open on this couch, but I don't know how long.

"Here," the girl kneels in front of me. She hands me a cup. "People said you got bad E and you were freaking out."

"Christine!" I say. I reach out to touch her hand. She doesn't mind; she touches back. I sip water from her cup. "I don't know if it was *bad* E," I mumble through wet lips. The water slides down my throat as if gravity just got doubled. "It *was* bad, though. I don't know. I never did it before."

Christine nods. "You don't look like you've done much."

"Yeah . . . at least it's, uh, better now. The world stopped shaking." *Hkkkk*, sputter; I drink more water. "You don't look like you've been having such a great time either."

"No." She shakes her head twice, very deliberately. Her eyes are red and streaked, but they're still dense and brown and beautiful. Her hair is still shiny.

"Sorry," I say, sitting up in one corner of the couch and scrunching my knees to my chest with the cup perched on top of them. The cup has Cupid on it. Maybe if I sit in one corner she'll sit in the other corner. "I'm sorry about Jake."

"Oh," she waves her hand, squatting on the floor. "That was like, way over. That was over two *days* ago. He can do whatever he wants with skanky girls in rooms while boys watch. ___ k ___ a_____ e."

I'm tired of Christine not being next to me, so I pat the couch to my left. She sits down. "He totally just started acting really weird a week ago. Like, he had layers to him. On the outside he seemed like a very confident high-school magnate, you know? You know what a magnate is?"

"Yes. Like a business guy." I look around the living room—it looks like winos have been fighting in here with baseball bats. There are liquor bottles strewn around and dents in the walls and ash and cigarette burns.

"Right. And then under that he had this whole other layer of sensitive, misunderstood wannabe-writer-type stuff, you know?"

"Jake's a writer?"

"He writes journals."

"Okay."

"But then the third layer was like his underlying evil *dick* layer."

"Ah."

"I mean, I couldn't believe it—you remember my system of stages?"

"Of course."

"Well, we went from Going Out to Him Just Being an Evil Dick really fast."

"Heh," I huff. "I thought you *came* with him tonight."

"No. I came by myself."

"Really? I went to the Halloween Dance by myself."

"You were there?" She inches closer. "I had no idea!"

"Yeah, for like forty minutes." How long ago was the Halloween Dance? A month? It seems like a month. A proper month of activity. I don't believe those people who say that "time goes so fast" and "your life is short." I'm bored enough that I always have a realistic sense of the actual, agonizing pace of a month. When you're in a room with no TV and just the Internet and not much homework and no friends, a month is a *month*. And this last month feels like a month, so full of unbelievable—

"Jeremy? Still with us?"

Right. "Sorry. I saw you dancing," I say.

"At the dance?"

"Yeah. You had that hat on, remember?"

"Oh, yeah . . . That's a traditional Sardinian princess hat. My mom made it out of linen. She's a historian."

"Oh." It's a good thing Christine didn't ask me what linen was, because I really don't know.

"What about you?" she continues. "I didn't see *you* dancing."

"I didn't."

Christine sighs. "You never do. Right?"

I nod.

"You nerdy boys, all the same." She kicks her heel against the couch and turns her head away, then back. "You're always so proud of what you *can't* do."

"That's not true!" I stand up. How did things turn out like this? Christine is here—and Jake isn't! This rocks. "I'm not happy I can't dance! I just can't! It's like a birth deficit! I mean defect!"

"That's not true," Christine says. "If you stopped thinking about yourself and just thought very academically about moving lightly so the girl could follow, you'd be fine."

"So come dance!" I beckon to her. I steady myself in the middle of the living room, shake my groin, close my eyes, bite my lip, put my hands on my hips and gyrate. Oh yeah.

"I'm tired," she dismisses. "Maybe some other time. There's no music."

"*Blukhuhuhuhuhuh*—" Laughter from across the room. "Shot *down*!" It's Rich, lounging on his own couch watching an infomercial set to mute, curiously without a girl on his stomach. There's a glass ashtray next to him on the floor with a cigarette in it. He looks up at me. "You two are *so-o-o* cute."

"Shut up, Rich." I turn to him. He throws the ashtray at me; I duck. The cigarette tumbles out and lies on the carpet while the ashtray hits a piano across the room, sounding middle C. (I used to take piano.) We all laugh.

I sit back on the couch with Christine, closer to her now. I like this—this late-party laid-back atmosphere, minus the music and the public sex and the angry jocks and the Spanish voice in my head. Somehow, like coming out of a tunnel, I've ended up with one person I really like and another—I look over at Rich—who I've kind of come to tolerate. Bombs have dropped and I'm happy in craters. I'm tired, though. I have to get home. I've got to start up—

HERE.

"You! Back in English!" I yell, getting up from the couch. Then I instantly sit back down as if nothing happened.

NICE ONE.

"What was that?" Christine asks, her eyes bugged.

"Rookie *mistake*!" Rich laughs, slapping his hand against his face. "Aw, you talked to your *squip*! Rookie mistake!"

YEAH. GOOD JOB. AND WE NEED TO TALK.

"Shut up," I hiss, sitting with my arms crossed, though I'm not sure who I'm talking to.

"What's yersquip?" Christine asks, looking at me.

"That's . . . my . . . imaginary . . . friend," I explain.

"Huh, yeah," Rich keeps laughing. "It's what he calls his p-penis."

"Would you shut up?" I throw a cushion at Rich.

"You have a name for your penis?" Christine asks. "Boys really *do* that?"

YEAH. RICH'S IS NAMED LI'L' CHEESE HEAD.

"Yeah. Rich's is named Li'l' Cheese Head," I say. Christine laughs and laughs and smiles, so I smile back at her. Rich throws his heavy shoe at me.

WE STILL NEED TO TALK.

"Uh, excuse me." I shinny out of the living room, duck the other shoe. "Back in a minute."

"Going to play with your imaginary friend?" Rich yells. Then: "Freak!"

But he says it with love.

I walk upstairs to the only bathroom I'm familiar with, the one where I saw Stephanie. I peek inside to make sure she hasn't returned. I close the door behind me and look at myself in the mirror. I do this at home; it's the easiest way to talk to the squip. Screw what it says—telepathy is hard on the brain.

"Okay, what do you want?" I stare at the mirror.

WHAT DO I WANT? WHAT DO *YOU* WANT? WHY DON'T YOU TELL ME? I'M JUST GETTING BACK UP TO SPEED AFTER A RUDE DRUG INTERRUPTION.

"Yeah, I caught that. You weren't too functional back there."

I TOLD YOU TO TURN ME OFF.

"Whatever. You have too many rules."

SO WHAT *DO* YOU WANT, JEREMY? CLEARLY, IT'S NOT TO GET LAID. I WORKED INCREDIBLY HARD TO GET YOU IN THE POSITION YOU WERE IN TONIGHT. I UTILIZED QUANTUM TELEPORTATION TO MINE OTHER SQUIPS FOR INFORMATION; I DELVED DEEP INTO MY OWN HUMAN MODELING ENGINES; I PLANNED DRIVING ROUTES, VERBAL ONE-LINERS, AND POINTS OF ATTACK ON THE FEMALE BODY; I SET YOU UP WITH A GIRL TO BRING YOU HERE AND A FEW BACKUPS IN CASE YOU MADE MISTAKES, AND I MADE SURE THEY WERE ALL, HANDS DOWN, THE MOST GORGEOUS FEMALES IN YOUR LIMITED UNIVERSE. AND YOU THREW IT ALL AWAY. SO WHAT? WHAT DO YOU WANT? ARE YOU REALLY GAY?

"No. I didn't throw it away. Bad things happened."

YOU COULD HAVE GOTTEN WITH STEPHANIE. AND

CHLOE . . . YOU SHOULDN'T HAVE TAKEN HER DRUGS. IF I HAD BEEN ON I WOULD HAVE TOLD YOU TO STAY OUT OF THAT BASEMENT. PROBABILITY AMPLITUDES WERE UNSTABLE IN THAT BASEMENT.

"Yeah, but see, this doesn't matter. Because I want Christine."

SO?

"That's it."

SO?

"That's who I like and that's who I want to be with, and when I think about it, that—I mean, *she*—is the reason I got *you* in the first place."

SO.

"So you are going to start listening to me, now, because I am the human being and I make the decisions and I don't care how many qubits you have or whatever because you are supposed to give *advice* like you said at the beginning!"

SO YOU WANT A COMPLETE PARADIGM SHIFT.

"I'm sorry?"

A COMPLETE SHIFT. A TOTAL MOVEMENT AWAY FROM WHAT YOU WANTED BEFORE. A NEW ANGLE. A NEW SET OF GOALS. A NEW DIRECTION FOR YOUR ENTIRELY PREDICTABLE AND MODELABLE LIFE. YOU NOW REJECT THE NOTIONS THAT YOU HAVE BEEN FED BY TELEVISION AND THONGS AND *XXX* THE MOVIE AND *XXX* ON THE INTERNET. YOU NOW WANT TO DEVOTE YOURSELF ENTIRELY TO THE CARE AND REDEMPTION OF CHRISTINE

Caniglia, who sets your heart aflame?

"Jesus. Are you still on drugs?"

No, you are. Am I right?

"Yes. I want to be with Christine and then I'll be happy."

Why do you need me, then?

"What?"

You've talked to her without me. You were just talking to her without me. My plans to win her affection haven't worked. Why not rely on yourself?

"Well, _h_ _."

What about it?

"You're my squip."

Yes.

"I need *you*. You've been here all along."

True. Off and on.

"I mean, I need your help. Advice. How to win her over. What to say. What kind of gifts to get her. When to make disapproving noises when she talks about which one of her friends. How to touch her. All the sexual stuff. I still need that, I think."

So you need me.

"Yes."

Then let's do this. And let's not waste time. *A Midsummer Night's Dream* opens in two weeks.

"Yeah."

By the time you do your bows, you'll be with Christine. I have a new plan.

"That's what I like to hear."

NOW, GET BACK TO THIS PARTY, OR WHAT'S LEFT OF IT. YOU'VE GOT UNFINISHED BUSINESS WITH MICHAEL, CHLOE, AND BROCK.

"_ _ _t, Brock."

DON'T WORRY. YOU'LL FIND HIM MORE DOCILE NOW. HE WON'T HIT YOU.

"I'm glad we cleared this up." I back away from the mirror and wink at myself.

YOU'RE STILL COOL.

thirty-
eight

When I return to the living room, Chloe and Brock are arm in arm, playing with each other's shirts. I guess they're back together; they look very right for one another. Brock's ponderous bulk nicely shadows Chloe's small curvaceousness.

"Jeremy, heyyyy," Chloe waves, struggling to stand. I guess she was smoking and drinking in addition to rolling, since she knew she had a ride home from me.

SHE WAS SNIFFING RITALIN.

Oh, great. "Hi, Chloe," I say, staying far away from Brock. "How are you?"

"Don't be worried about Brock or anything," Chloe says. "I _ _c_ _ _ him, so he's happy now. He's my boyfriend again."

Brock smiles. "Yeah, sorry for chasing you, dude. This girl." He strokes Chloe's cheek and they kiss, facing Christine on her couch, with their butts pointed at Rich on his couch.

"Turn around!" Rich yells. "I want to see you lick her tongue! I'm bored."

Brock and Chloe keep kissing, but that doesn't stop Brock from sticking his hand out for me to slap it, a gesture of solidarity. I can't believe *this* happy ending, either.

HOW COME YOU'RE SURPRISED BY MALE BEHAVIOR?

I'm sorry?

DON'T YOU SEE THAT THIS IS HOW MEN INTERACT? THEY STAGE FIGHTS WITH ONE ANOTHER TO DETERMINE WHOM THEY CAN CONTROL. WHEN A FIGHT ENDS IN AN UNEXPECTED WAY, THEY FIND THEMSELVES WITH AN EQUAL OR SUPERIOR INSTEAD OF AN UNDERLING. THEN, OUT OF FEAR, THEY BEFRIEND THE PERSON WHO BESTED THEM. YOU BEAT BROCK, SO NOW YOU GET TO BE HIS FRIEND. SEE?

Oh. I slap Brock's hand dutifully.

BUT FORGET THESE TWO. GO OVER TO CHRISTINE AND OFFER HER A RIDE HOME.

"Christine?" I ask. "Do you want a ride home? I'm going to give Chloe and, uh, I guess Brock a ride." I shrug my elbow at them.

"You're okay to drive?" she asks, looking up from whatever she had in her lap and hiding it. But I saw it: a worn, highlighted copy of the *Midsummer Night's Dream* script, folded in quarters.

WORK THAT.

"Wait, you're doing your lines now?" I ask. I put the emphasis on *lines* instead of *now* to make it friendly.

"Yeah, shh." She puts a finger to her lips. "I'm a serious dork about this play."

"Me too." I move closer to her. No. DON'T BE SALACIOUS. I move away. "We can go over some scenes in my car. And I am okay to drive," I reassure her.

"Uh . . . I can't even believe you have a car, Jeremy. I didn't know you *could* drive."

"How do you think I got here?"

"Huh." She dips her head down, then up. "How come you don't drive to school?"

EXERCISE.

"Exercise." I stretch.

"Well, are you ready to go? It is like three in the morning. I was going to call up a car service. I have to do the whole sneaking-into-my-house thing."

"Me too." I stand up. "Okay. Chloe and, uh, I assume you too Brock"—he nods—"head out to the lawn. I'm going to find Michael Mell and then we're all out of here. I'll drop everybody off where they need to be."

"Jeremy Heere, taking charge like a big boy," Rich smirks. "Good luck with that full load of heads, man. You okay to drive?"

YES.

"Yes."

"All right. See ya," Rich slaps my hand. Chloe and Brock walk out to the lawn (they *listened* to me); Christine and I delve back into the party-sore house to find Michael.

"This is that guy with the 'fro, right?" she asks. "The one you're always hanging out with?"

"Yeah. He's, like, my best friend, y'know—if I could still say 'best friend.'" We walk down the hall with our hands pocketed. "I guess now that I'm older I'm supposed to call him something else."

AT LEAST YOU'RE NOT CALLING HIM "BUDDY." THAT'S HIGHLY UNDESIRABLE.

"Best friend is fine," Christine says. "Girls use best friend till they're, like, *dead*."

"Okay," I smile.

We do a random room check, opening doors on kids lying in their own puke, crying, drinking beer out of ashtrays, sleeping or playing Kill All People in a sedentary frenzy. In each room we ask for "Michael" and an impostor Michael turns around, deadened by the sound of his own name, burned out. It seems like a lot of kids (and a special contingent of Michaels) are staying at the Finderman house tonight—Jason Finderman's parents must really be in Barbados. It's like the Land Without Parents, a Lost World.

TELL THAT TO CHRISTINE.

"It's like *Lord of the Flies* in here," I say as we leave a room that had a bunch of jocks standing in a circle chanting and pumping their fists at another jock doing one-armed push-ups on the floor.

"I was thinking the exact same thing," she says. "Do parties always get this *weird* when it's late?"

I await instruction from the squip. TELL THE TRUTH.

"I don't know. I've never really been to a serious party before."

"Me neither!" Christine grins. She grabs my shoulder just for a second. "Me neither."

We're upstairs. I peek into one door while Christine tries another. "Hey, is that him?"

She's looking inside a bathroom—one I didn't know about, without a crazy self-abusing Hot Girl inside. This room has party scars: the sink is full of what appears to be shaving cream; someone has tagged FROG: MY BIZNESS IS OUT OF THIS BIZNICH in permanent marker above the toilet, and in the bathtub, Michael Mell is covered with a small Asian girl, who's wearing a towel. They look asleep. Michael's afro is compromised by the back of the tub.

"Michael," I hiss. "It's me!"

"Wuh?" He looks up, eyes disturbingly white. Then his irises and pupils rotate out of his skull and his face lights up. "Dude! Look! Isn't she beautiful?"

I try to make a judgment about the compact and somewhat oily-looking lump who lies on Michael; all I can think is that she's got black, short hair and her arms are plump and she's very asleep.

"She's snow_bunny," Michael says.

"From where?" I know that's a username.

"Raptalk-dot-net, this, uh, underground hip-hop board," he admits. "She's a moderator there."

"I thought you hated rap."

"Yeah. Well. I still do." ·

"What's her real name?"

"Nicole. Snow_bunny was how she introduced herself to me, though. I was trying to change that horrible music in the den. We had a connection."

"This house has a den?" Christine asks from the sink. "I always wanted a den."

"Who's . . ." Michael squints. "Whoa, it's Christine!" He turns his chin up to me. "You got—"

"*Eccch . . .*" I warn, pinching his shoulder. Hard.

"Right. Hi Christine!" he nods. "I'd wave but my arms are pinned."

"Hi," she waves, bending her elbow but keeping the rest of her arm rigid. It's a cute wave. "I want to see the den."

"No. We're staying together." I kneel down to Michael's level. "You want a ride home?"

"Well, yeah. I need to get my car back, remember?"

Jeez. That seems like it happened last *year*. "Wake her up then, man. We're going."

"All right." Michael shifts into a more upright position. "Nicole, wake up."

"*Muh,*" the girl mumbles.

"I think you guys had better wait outside. I'll get her out of the tub," Michael plans. Christine and I exit and sit in the hall, cross-legged on the carpet, knees at a safe distance, facing the bathroom door. From inside we hear banging, scraping, gargling, and male and female murmurs. I try to think of something to say.

No. Keep quiet.

Why?

You talk to this girl too much, Jeremy. You're acceptable around guys and most girls, but with this one, you talk until the blood vessels in your head expand and cramp me. You need to give it a rest. Get that air of mystery about you.

So I sit. Every time I almost talk (about a half-dozen times), the squip shuts me up. After three minutes, shockingly, Christine breaks out with something: "I f_ _k_ _ _ can't believe Jake." She shakes her head and pushes stray hair over her ears. "I don't even want to say this because it's so stupid, but I thought he really *liked* me."

Hand on her shoulder. Firm. Friendly.

"He's a dick," I reassure. "We're all dicks, if you give us the chance. We're just guys. We react to threats and rewards."

"Yeah?"

I pull my hand away, gesticulate with it. I'm feeling smart. "Sure. For a guy, there's something dangling in front of your face or something sticking out your ass." What a brilliant analysis. OH DEF-INITELY. "That's what we care about."

"So I have to put something in his *ass*?" Christine says, horrified. "That's what you want? I heard about that, the prostate—"

"No, I just meant . . . uh . . ."

"I don't want to have to wear a strap-on, Jeremy!" And she leans down, unexpectedly, into my lap. I'm about to laugh because this is pretty stupid, but she's far from laughing, she's choking in small gasps as if she's been waiting all night for an excuse to cry. Her tears wet my pants. I put my hand down carefully.

HAIR ONLY.

I make light strokes. And instead of being derisive, I'm nice/funny. "You know, this whole millennium is going to be the Millennium of the Woman," I say. (She sniffles.) "So you're not going to have to worry about guys like Jake."

"Yeah?"

"Oh yeah. I read about it in *Time* magazine. I'm very happy with it. I'd rather live in a world run by women."

Christine smiles and the very beginning of a laugh ripples her throat.

"They could, like, lust after me and touch my butt while I was trying to photocopy stuff at my job and I'd be like, 'Ha-ha, stop that, ladies.'"

"Yeah, right."

"And then they'd hound me and try to get photographs of me in my underwear and I'd have to hire security and have them sign up for whenever they wanted to see me, like only on Wednesday nights—"

"Jeremy, 'Millennium of the Woman' doesn't mean that."

"No?"

"No. It just means we get *paid* as much as you do."

"Oh, you're never gonna get paid as much as me. I got my sights set high in this world."

"Yeah? Where?"

"Photocopy guy."

"Jeremy! That's not a job!" Christine isn't teary anymore. She lifts herself up.

"Course it is. My dad says that at every job there's one guy who just messes around with the photocopy machine."

"Jeremy, computers, remember? We're not going to need copy machines soon."

YES. DUH.

"Then I can hang around the *coffee* machine."

"Those aren't jobs, Jeremy."

ASK FOR HER NUMBER.

Why now?

BECAUSE YOU'RE DOING WELL NOW. AND IN A FEW SECONDS, MICHAEL AND NICOLE ARE GOING TO COME OUT OF THAT BATHROOM AND YOU'RE ALL GOING TO GET IN YOUR

"Christine." I shrug intensely. "Can I have your
number so I can call you sometime? We can talk
about the millennium and . . . whatever." There's an
unfinished gap. What didn't I say? "Please."

"Eh." She shrugs and backs away, then leans forward just enough to give me hope. "You have to
promise never to be a dick like Jake."

"Okay."

"And also not to call me all the time or embarrass
me in school or treat me any different than you do
now."

"Right."

"And when I give out a number, it's not my signal
that I'm going to have sex with you. We're still
friends, okay?"

"Agreed."

"Really agreed?"

"Really. Agreed."

"Then fine," she says, and gives it to me. Over the
squip's protests, I write this precious piece of information down on an actual piece of paper.

thirty-nine

We cram into Mom's Maxima the way teenagers are supposed to cram into their parents' cars. Michael and Nicole share a lap in the back ("Your butt is really comfortable," Michael says, "it's too bad *you* can't sit on it . . . wait"); she wears a kiddie-size T-shirt, bringing to the forefront some assets that weren't evident in the bathtub. Brock occupies two seats next to Michael, and Chloe lies on top of Brock with her head in Nicole's lap, telling her how pretty she is. I look in the rearview mirror and nod at Michael. She *is* pretty. She has a pretty face. He nods back at me. Christine rides shotgun. I start the car.

IT'S TOO BAD THERE'S NO STICKSHIFT. YOU COULD BRUSH YOUR HAND AGAINST HER IF YOU HAD A STICKSHIFT. SHE'D NOTICE SUBCONSCIOUSLY.

That's a terrible idea. I power down my window so the cold air—black air—rushes over me, keeping me awake as we pull away from the Finderman house.

The clock says 3:37, which is not as late as I imagined, but I'm still tired as hell.

I CAN STIMULATE PARTS OF YOUR BRAIN TO KEEP YOU UP.

Really? Which parts?

RETICULAR FORMATION. LINES YOUR BRAINSTEM.

Oh.

IT'S EASY. I SEND IT A CONTROLLED ELECTRICAL SIGNAL; IT RELEASES NOREPINEPHRINE AND YOU STAY SCARED AND AWAKE.

Do it. I don't feel anything, but my eyes spring open and stay that way. I drive fast but still in control. I wonder how fast I'm going; I look down to see a disappointing 50—

WATCH!

I jerk my head up—a fire truck barrels past in the other direction. I get a flash of calm, burly men inside and watch in the mirror as the red lights fade to a distant spot. "Jesus."

HOW MANY TIMES DO WE HAVE TO DO THIS? NOT "JESUS." "FU_K."

"Can we listen to music?" Michael whines, leaning forward.

"No. I'm trying to concentrate."

"That's because you never drove before," Michael chuckles. He's drunk. YES. "If you'd driven before, you might understand that music helps you. . . ." He reaches forward with a CD.

"No!" Nicole says to him. "C'mon, not rock!"

"Damn it, Michael!" I punch his wrist while gripping the wheel. CAREFUL, CAREFUL. AND "DAMN IT?" "I don't want to *listen* to anything now!"

Eoooooowwwwwww—another fire truck rumbles past. Full speed. We almost hit it, and the car shifts to the left in its wake, sliding a foot toward the other side of the road. Everybody shuts up. I keep my foot steady on the accelerator, putting a safe distance between us and the truck. Then I turn to Christine: "So, you want to go over those *Midsummer* lines still?"

"Cue me," she says mechanically. Her arms are folded over her seat belt. I'm not wearing my seat belt.

OF COURSE NOT.

"C'mon, cue me," Christine insists.

"Uh . . ." I try to think of a cue for Puck.

IT'S A TRAP.

"You can't, see?" she says. "Lysander doesn't *cue* Puck. Ever. So I guess you should concentrate on driving."

"Ur."

For the next ten minutes, nobody says a word except Christine, mutely giving directions to her house. When we get there, I park as leisurely as I can in front of her lawn.

"Jeremy?"

"Yeah?"

"Could you pull up more so I don't have to open the door into my own garbage?"

Plastic bins wait outside Christine's house for the sanitation guys, who I guess will show up in an hour.

"Right, okay." I pull the car up a little, stop again. "Is that good?" WALK HER IN. "I'll walk you in."

Christine stays silent. I leave the car in neutral, step out and stride over to her side. She's already out, walking around the edge of her lawn to her house. I start after her, rubbing my arms. It's *cold* out here.

STOP. THERE ARE MOTION SENSORS. YOU'LL TURN ON A BIG FLOODLIGHT IF YOU STEP ONTO THE LAWN.

I plant my feet. "Chri—"

WHISPER. AND SAY "TH" FOR "S," LIKE YOU HAD A LISP. THE SOUND DOESN'T CARRY SO FAR.

"Uh . . . *Chrithtine*," I hiss, feeling like an idiot. "I'll call you . . . uh . . . thoon."

"When you call me you'd better actually know how to drive," she seethes, wisely picking a sentence with no s's. Then she turns away in the night.

THIS GIRL. VERY DIFFICULT.

I stand and watch her, just a butt and legs and arms, receding into the black. How come they're so compelling?

BECAUSE THEY PRODUCE CHILDREN.

Come on.

AND THEY MOTIVATE YOU. THEY DEFINE YOU, REALLY. THEY MAKE YOU HUMAN.

I trudge back to the car.

HUMAN!

And then the squip does something I haven't heard before: it laughs. It's horrible. Keanu Reeves laughing in your mind? Must be what schizos hear.

Everyone stays quiet as I drive to Chloe's house next. I say cordial good-byes to her and Brock (Chloe kisses my cheek; Brock slaps my hand); then Michael and Nicole space out in back, lounging for the final leg of the trip. When we pull up to my house, I notice with extreme horror that the kitchen light is on. That could mean Dad forgot to turn it off or it could mean he stayed up two hours later than usual watching the History Channel *(Secrets of the Nazis, Nazis and the Occult, Hitler's Last Nazis)* or it could mean he's waiting for me with his fists clenched. He's never hit me, but I *am* in his wife's car. How am I going to handle this?

TAKE MICHAEL'S CAR OUT OF THE DRIVEWAY YOURSELF, WITH NO ENGINE, AS YOU DID WITH YOUR MOM'S CAR AT THE BEGINNING OF THE NIGHT. THEN PUT YOUR MOM'S CAR BACK SLOWLY AND QUIETLY.

"Give me your keys, man," I reach back to Michael. He hands them over; I bunch them up in my fist, turn off the car and step out. I crawl on my hands and knees up my own driveway, open the passenger door of Michael's ride, squirm across the canyon between the two front seats, release the emergency brake and wait for his car to slide down the driveway. It doesn't.

IT'S TOO HEAVY. OLDER CAR. BIGGER ENGINE UP FRONT. YOU'RE GOING TO HAVE TO PUSH.

_ _c_. I crawl back down the driveway and inform Michael. "Why can't you just start it and back it up?" he asks.

"Because I can't wake my dad, genius, and your car is noisy as hell. Get out and help."

"I'll help too," Nicole offers. "This one's too skinny." She hits Michael.

"I'm good-skinny, though," Michael says. We all sneak up the driveway; then, like a crack Olympic team in a new sport, we grab ahold of Michael's front bumper in synchronization. "What kind of car ith thith, anyway?" I whisper.

"Ford Crown Victoria. One of the heaviest, most gluttonous vehicles ever constructed. What's wrong with your voice?"

"Nevermind." I position myself in the middle of the fender, arch my fingers under it and try to brace my legs on the asphalt—I'm glad my driveway's not gravel. "All right, ready?" I turn right and then left, judging my compatriots. Nicole looks determined, like one of those people who have to move a car in the World's Strongest Man competition, but Michael's arms (he rolled his sleeves up) are even scrawnier than I remembered.

"One . . . two . . . *Ungggh*." I throw my weight forward,

trying to pull the mass after me as I lean over the hood. The insides of my knuckles pinch the fender and burn. My arms ripple. I think the car's moving—

SHIFT LEFT.

I pull my hands off the fender for a second—the car dips noticeably toward me—and reapply them a foot to the left. There's a little creak, like a hamster wheel, as the car starts moving back, centimeter by centimeter. I can hear each tire tread contact the road with a squish.

THAT'S IT! BEFORE YOU HAD TOO MUCH FORCE ON THE RIGHT SIDE; NOW YOU'RE MAKING UP FOR MICHAEL! KEEP GOING!

Rrrrragh! Blood vessels pound me from inside.

ENDORPHIN RELEASE. SYMPATHETIC NERVOUS SYSTEM.

I'm fiery and in control as I beat the car's center of gravity and start it rolling down the driveway.

"Oh _ _ _ _," Michael says as the car slips away. I abandon my post at left-center and scramble around the hood, trying to keep a hand on it at all times. I clang open the passenger door, leap inside, sprawl across the two front seats and reach for the brake as the slope of the driveway pulls the car down. I hope I parked Mom's car clear of the driveway—a collision would mean certain death at the hands of Dad or Mom or both. I finally get the brake, the one you're supposed to use your feet on, and flex my fingers as the car moves faster and faster—

It stops.

I poke my head up, then start laughing. I'm in the middle of the street. The car almost went clear across Rampart Road into the yard of Crazy Bill, our neighbor. There's no telling what he would have done had I disturbed his garbage sculptures at four in the morning. Michael is doubled over with laughter in the driveway, but Nicole looks concerned; she bounces across the road and opens the door on me, exhausted, panting in the passenger seat.

"You a'ight?" she asks.

THIS GIRL WANTS YOU.

"Yeah."

"That was really cool. I've never seen anybody do that. You were fast."

"Heh." I look up at her, my eyes lidded just the right way, with my hand on my thigh and sweat on the bridge of my nose. I could do her now if I wanted. Right?

YEAH.

"You seem like a nice girl," I say. "Take care of my friend."

Nicole shrugs as Michael approaches. "Dude, that was spectacular. I had no idea you were an action hero."

"Only on Tuesdays." I get out of the car. Someone once told me that that's what you should say when people ask if you're a millionaire.

I TOLD YOU THAT.

Oh.

"Four-o-five," Michael looks at his watch. "Gotta take this car home."

Nicole slides into the passenger seat: "I'm choosing music!" she says, waving her MP3 player out the window. "No rock!" Michael shakes his head; he can bring Nicole home if he wants; his mom doesn't care. He walks past me to get to the driver's seat.

"You did good," I say quietly, slapping his hand.

"We did good," he says. "You're doing great with Christine. You two are cute."

"We will be."

"So we get girls? Who woulda thunk." Michael takes his keys from me and turns on the Crown Victoria, making a slow right in the middle of the street. "Peace!" he and Nicole say. She puts one foot out the window and leans on Michael as they drive away.

He's never said "peace" before. HE'S COMING ALONG. I pull Mom's car into the driveway without incident—its motor is quieter than Michael's car's—and go into my house as silently as I can, which is pretty silent—the squip tells me which parts of the porch creak. Dad isn't even in the kitchen; he's asleep on the couch as usual. I didn't have to go through all that crap to try and not wake him. But it was fun.

forty

NEWS FLASH, the squip declares.

I'm cronked out in bed on my stomach, with my shoes on. All I want is sleep. But it's the same flatly urgent tone the squip used when Eminem died.

NEWS FLASH.

"Wha-ut?" I roll over, lazy. I pry my shoes off with my heels and let them flop to the floor.

THERE WAS A FIRE. RICH GOT EXTREMELY BADLY BURNED.

"What?" I sit straight up.

THERE WAS A FIRE. RICH GOT EXTREMELY BADLY BURNED. The repetition is exact, uncharacteristic, a bug in the software or something. Maybe—

NO. NO BUGS. RICH SUFFERED CRITICAL BURNS. PART OF THE FINDERMAN HOUSE CAUGHT ON FIRE, JUST AFTER YOU LEFT. I THOUGHT YOU SHOULD KNOW BEFORE THE REST OF THE WORLD. IT HAPPENED IN THE LAST HALF HOUR.

I look at the clock. It's 4:17. You're for real? He's in the hospital?

INTENSIVE CARE.

In this universe?

YES.

And the house was on *fire*?

WELL. NOT ALL OF IT.

What the f_c_? What am I supposed to say to that?

PROBABLY "NO, NO, THIS CAN'T BE HAPPENING?"

"This can't be *happening*!" I get out of bed and walk in a horseshoe pattern around my room. I've never had any of my friends or family get seriously hurt, not even pets, because Dad hates pets and thinks that people who keep them are weak. My grandparents are all alive and everything. I reach for the phone.

WHO ARE YOU CALLING? DON'T CALL ANYONE!

"I was going to call Christine."

BAD IDEA. TALK TO ME!

"How—did you know it was going to happen?"

IT WAS A DISTINCT POSSIBILITY. THERE WAS A LOT OF FLAME IN THAT HOUSE. PROBABILITY AMPLITUDES WERE BAD TOO, AS I SAID. NOT JUST IN THE BASEMENT.

"Could we have stopped it?"

I'M NOT A SUPERHERO, JEREMY. NEITHER ARE YOU.

"How come his squip didn't stop it?"

COMMUNICATION PARAMETERS WEREN'T RESPECTED. SUBSTANCES.

I sit back on the bed. For not much reason except I know it's what I'm supposed to do and it's late and I can't think to do anything else and I have this buttery feeling in my stomach, I cry.

You don't need to.

"Why?" I snort into my palms. "Do you know how messed up this is?"

It's not that bad.

"*Not that bad?* Even from a practical standpoint, it's gonna be, like, all over school. All the parents are going to want to know what was going on in that house and it's gonna be like a police investigation . . . what else happened?"

Jake Dillinger is in the hospital with burns as well.

"Jake *Dillinger?* _ _ _k! Why didn't you tell me that before?"

Data-rationing is turned on. Would you like it off?

"No, this is enough. . . . Oh man, it'll be speeches and counseling and everything."

It'll be a good time to talk to Christine.

"*Shut up!* Don't say that!"

Why?

"Because two people are in the hospital. You have to have respect when people are in the hospital or when they die or something."

Why?

"Because you do. . . ."

You didn't have much respect when Eminem died.

"He's a celebrity! He's *supposed* to die!"

You have bad parents, you know that?

"Why?" I get up, pace, sit down again.

They should have prepared you for situations like this. I'm not programmed to counsel human shock and sorrow. I'm more about results.

I slump back in bed and think about Rich—Jake too a little bit, but I don't think about Jake so much because the last time I saw him he was just two feet in a room of sex, while the last time I saw Rich he was smiling at me. I think about how no matter how cool Rich got, he returned to his dork roots at the end, throwing that ashtray at me and whining, alone on a couch.

Oh man. The ashtray. He was drunk with his squip on. That couldn't have been good. Rich had had a squip for months; he was probably experimenting with it, seeing what it could take.

Probably so.

F_ _k. I ask the squip for help and it drops my synapses off into sleep, but it can't control my dreams: Rich all charred up, making fun of me, with no face, holding his head out for me to slap it like a hand, with a pill swimming in alcohol inside.

forty-
one

My phone rings at 8:30 the next day. It's Michael. "Holy s___ holy _h__ holy __i_," he runs. "Did I wake you up?"

"Yeah," I wheeze.

"Hello?" Mom chirps, answering the phone downstairs. She knows that I've answered—there was a lot of time after that last ring—so she's just trying to infiltrate my life.

TRUE.

"Mom, it's for me."

"Oh, you're *up*, Jeremy! We need to talk—"

"Mom, can I have, like, five minutes?"

"O-o-o-kay. You were out *very late*," she admonishes. She hangs up. Michael has hardly breathed while she's been on the line. "It burned, man; the Finderman house burned. Somebody tried to smoke pot near the basement tank or something and one side of the house—*fffshsshoo*."

"I had a feeling."

"You did?"

"Yeah."

"What, did you *do* it?"

"No. There were fire trucks, remember?"

"Oh _ _ck."

"Yeah, those fire trucks that went past at, like, eighty while I was driving for the second time in my life and you were stupid-highway-drunk with Nicole . . ."

"Jeremy, I'm sorry, but Nicole's really cool—"

A click comes through the receiver again. "Jeremy?" Mom. "I'm sorry to bother you; have you seen your father's car keys?"

F _ _ _, they're still in my pocket!

TELL HER NO.

"No, Mom," I say. "Let me just finish up with Michael."

She clicks off: "O-o-o-kay."

"Listen, man," I continue, quickly, but Michael has a question: "Did anyone die?" he asks. "I heard Rich died."

"No! He's in intensive care."

"How do you know?"

CHRISTINE.

"I talked to Christine just before you."

"You did? Well that's good; I'm kinda freaked out about the whole thing; do you want to come over? I have to tell you about Nicole."

NOT NECESSARY. HANDLE THE KEYS.

"No, but thanks," I mumble. "We'll talk. He's not dead." Right?

YES.

"Okay. Bye." Michael gets off the phone.

LEAVE THEM IN THE BATHROOM.

I hurry in, pee sitting down, splash water on my face (my eyes look swampy), drop the keys nonchalantly by the toilet and rush back to my room. I write a bold note with a Sharpie and tack it to my door (DO NOT DISTURB—THE MANAGEMENT), slide into bed (it hits me all at once—I'm even more tired than last night), pick up the phone and sheepishly dial the number that I have stored in my pocket.

NO!

"Hello?"

"Hi, Christine," I speed through the words. "It's Jeremy. I just wanted to tell you in case you didn't hear that last night after we left there was this—"

"It's not Christine. It's her mother."

"Oh."

"Do you know what time it is? Please don't call this early." Click.

"The keys!" Mom yells from the bathroom.

JEREMY, SLEEP MORE.

Yeah. I should. The world isn't in sync with me yet. I close my eyes for what I want to be an hour, but when I open them because of some noise, instead of streaming in the way it was doing in the morning, the light in my room is just *there*, shaming me. My arm is draped over my face to protect my eyes against it.

Brrrrring. The phone is ringing again. I pick it up while lying down. "Hmeh?"

"Jeremy?" A girl's voice.

"Mrrrph." Christine? YES. "Christine! How'd you get my number?"

"Caller ID, of course," she says. "From you calling here at like eight-thirty in the morning. What's up? Are you okay?"

"Holy crap, no," I slap my face.

THAT'S GOOD. DON'T CURSE WITH HER. IT'S 12:30 P.M., FOR YOUR INFO.

"I'm very disturbed."

She sighs. "I thought you would be."

"So you heard?" I sit up. This girl calms me.

"Wait, first, why did you call my house so early?"

TELL THE TRUTH.

"I . . . uh . . . I just wanted to talk to you about the whole fire thing."

"That's sweet. How did you find out about it? Who told you?"

MICHAEL.

"Michael did. He saw it on the way, driving back to his house." I feel bad about lying.

DON'T. IT'S NECESSARY.

"Well," she says. "We don't get too many phone calls before nine A.M. on a Sunday."

"Must've pissed your mom off."

"She'll live."

"Yeah, maybe she thought it was one of her eight-A.M. booty calls."

"Shut *up*!" Christine laughs. Then we both realize what we should be talking about.

"So, uh, the fire thing is super messed up," I offer. "What did you hear about it?"

"Everything," she says. "Too much. Let's talk about something else."

"Uh . . ."

EMBARRASSING PARENTAL DETAILS. BORING YET SAFE.

"My Dad eats Peanut Butter Oreos *dipped in peanut butter*."

"*Waa!* He must be kind of . . . ah . . ."

"Large? Yeah, he's large. He's gotten large lately."

"My dad goes on business trips and comes back with all the peanuts from the airplanes, including other people's peanuts, for me."

"Why?"

"He remembers how much I used to like them when I was little. I don't even eat them anymore."

"Is he away a lot?"

"Great Adventure has these strategy meetings in Vegas. He goes there. And he has miles from his old job that he uses to visit family."

"I'd miss my dad if he was away all the time," I say, out of bed now, pacing.

Stop pacing. It adds a tremor to your voice. And what are you doing?

"Me too." Christine says. "I do. But he sends letters, you know? Not e-mails, real letters with stamps that you have to actually buy."

"Huh," I laugh.

There's a pause. Interesting. We're learning a lot here.

I know!

"You still there, Jeremy?"

"Yeah. Sorry."

"You know, you and I and Brock and Chloe and Michael are really lucky." (I don't say anything. I'm noticing how close I was to her in the sentence.) "We owe you a lot, actually. You were the one that rushed us out of that house."

"I was tired," I say, putting boxers on, exceedingly careful not to hang up the phone as it nestles between my chin and shoulder. "I wanted to go home."

"Isn't it weird that that's the kind of stuff that saves you from being hurt?" she asks. "Being tired?"

"Yeah. Life is very random."

Like a quantum computer.

"Like a quantum computer."

"Like what?"

"Stupid," I hiss at the squip. AH, LEAVE ME ALONE.

"Jeremy?" CALL HER "BEAUTIFUL GIRL." NOW.

"Yes, beautiful girl?"

"Stop it." Christine blushes over the phone. I knew that could happen. Then she says, "I forgot what I was going to say."

YOU WERE GOING TO SAY THAT WE SHOULD MEET UP TO GO OVER OUR LINES EVEN THOUGH LYSANDER NEVER TALKS TO PUCK AND PUCK NEVER TALKS TO LYSANDER.

"You were going to say that we should meet up to go over lines even though Lysander never talks to Puck and Puck never talks to Lysander—you just throw dust at me."

"Jeremy, don't you think we could just talk on the phone a little while? Like, not so pushy. Remember what I asked you?"

"All right." And with the help of the squip and my own quick thinking, Christine and I manage to have an actual conversation about movies and our friend(s) and how screwed up the whole fire thing is and how hurt Rich is and what school is going to be like and the play and how Jake Dillinger is a dick anyway even if he's in the hospital and Mr. Reyes and climate change and parents and homework. NO, NOT HOMEWORK, the squip says when I get there. TALKING ABOUT HOMEWORK IS A FIRST STEP ON THE PATH TO EUNUCH-HOOD. I switch.

The conversation goes so well that I'm surprised,

forty-five minutes in, to have the squip order an ending. BE THE TERMINATOR. SHOW THAT YOUR ESSENCES ARE PRIZED IN THIS WORLD, it says. "I gotta go deal with my parents," I say. "I assume they've heard everything by now."

"They're gonna be crazy," Christine says. "Like mine."

"Well, then, it'll be fun."

"Definitely. Bye, Jeremy." She lilts her voice in an exceedingly pleasant manner.

"Have a good one," I almost say. But the squip corrects me: ANOTHER RUNG ON THE EUNUCH LADDER. STICK WITH "PEACE."

"Peace," I slur, and right on cue, Mom raps on my door. Maybe she was standing outside, waiting for me to end the call.

"Jeremy, we have to talk *right now* about where my car was last night and what happened to your aunt's Beanie Babies!"

forty-two

I crumble into a subordinate chair at the dining room table. Mom and Dad are centurions, in established positions. She's at the head of the table and he's behind her, sitting on a radiator in a Godfather-type pose. (I've never seen *The Godfather* . . . I've seen the *Sopranos*, though—good enough?) He looks like he should be in charge quietly from the background, but I know he's probably just eating over there by the oval garbage can. This is Mom's show. I look up at her.

"First things first," she says. "We heard about the fire at the Finderman house last night. That's where you were, right?"

"Yeah."

"Well, are you okay?" Mom looks at me deeply.

"Yeah. I left before all that stuff happened. You know, whatever happened."

"Okay," Mom says. Then, as if they've been planning it all morning, she and Dad approach and hug me in sequence. I hug back, almost crying the way I did last night, into Dad's big body. "We're happy you're safe," he says gruffly. The hug is long and tight.

My parents return to their positions. Mom has her hands on the back of the main dining room chair like a boat wheel. I notice that she's wearing a very businesslike, nonweekend outfit. She adopts a serious expression: "Now, I have some questions. Are you on drugs."

No. Not now.

"No, not now."

"Don't be smart with me, Jeremy." Mom approaches. "What happened at that party last night? What were you doing that kept you up until four in the morning?"

"Nothing." No. Tell the truth. "Well . . . some stuff . . ."

"What? Likewhatstuff?" Mom leans forward. It's easy to forget that your mother is a lawyer until it counts.

Tell her everything.

What do you mean?

Tell her everything. She's smart. It's the only way to get out of this.

But—

Jeremy, aren't we past arguing?

"I did ecstasy. . . ." I mumble.

"*Hu-aaaa!*" Mom grabs me. "You did? Did some-one force you to?"

Dad laughs his ass off. "Did someone *force* him?" A sandwich quivers in his mouth. "Whoa, huh, yeah, *right.*"

"No, nobody forced me," I stare ahead. Mom puts her hands tight around my cheeks, pulling my face up at her, and holds me there. "I just tried it. I'm young. I'm stupid."

"Jeremy, what is wrong with you?" She looks at me so deeply that I think my body might straighten up to accommodate her gaze, from eyes to toes. "What is this?" She holds up a credit card bill, with the shirt I bought at Advanced Horizons highlighted (I have to stare close to see it). "Why are you abusing our credit card?"

"*Mguph.*" I answer. Mom still holds my mouth shut.

"Why is my sister missing hundreds of dollars worth of Beanie Babies?"

"Yeah!" Dad seconds, hearing his cue. "I *saw* you looking at those gay things on the Internet. What have you been doing on the Internet?"

Mom looks back and sighs. "Why was my car parked differently in the driveway this morning than it was last night?" she asks. "Why are there sixteen more miles on it?"

Jeez—she checks that stuff?

Your Mom is really mental. Tell the truth.

"Because I took it to the party."

"You took my car to the party! *Why would you do that?*"

I've never seen my mother jump up and down before, but I've also never ever seen anything resembling the remotest, tiniest body of water create any kind of reflection in her eyeballs. Until now.

"When did I lose my son?" Mom goes from jumping to kneeling. She's below me now, tearing up. "When?" She touches my leg.

Tell her about me.

What?

It's the only way.

She won't—

Tell her.

"I, uh . . ." Mom looks at me plaintively. "I got a quantum computer that I ate and now it sits in my brain and tells me how to be cool. And it changed me."

"Oh my gosh."

I don't say anything.

"He's insane. Your son has gone insane." Mom turns to Dad. "Now we have to get him a specialist and everything."

"I'm *sane*!" I stand up. This isn't something I ever thought I'd have to defend.

You're doing fine.

"I'm really sane!"

"Jeremy, we don't need to talk about this right now. I want you to go to your room and lie down and take some aspirin or . . . whatever you need to do to get those drugs out of your system. Your father and I are going to have a discussion and come up with a game plan to get you the help you need." Now Mom is crying, and I learn something I didn't know about the human body: if your mom cries, you cry. So there we are, her bawling and me with my auto-bawl feature activated, together at the dining room table; me trying to explain that I just did the ecstasy once and I'm not lying about the squip and Mom holding my head and wondering out loud where she went wrong and telling me that she loves me so much, her only son, at least I wasn't burned in the fire.

forty-
three

I'm back in school on Monday. It's not like you can
ignore the fact that there was a tragedy and some
people got put in the hospital and a member of the
community's house burned, because right over
the entrance, on a big banner put together to look like
a quilt, the school administrators have written: WE
ARE MIDDLE BOROUGH.

"We are Middle Borough?" Isn't that what they
wrote at Columbine after those two kids shot all
those other kids?

THEY WROTE "WE ARE COLUMBINE."

Well, duh. But weren't we Middle Borough before?

APPARENTLY NOT.

I walk through the doors. Since there's no Rich
standing outside, there's no group for me to hang out
with before class. I just head in the way I used to, alone
and thinking about school, instead of with a group of
people, thinking about how I can please/use them.

Inside, instead of walking purposefully, wearing their pastiche of name brands, students are standing in medium-size circles by lockers of importance: Rich's locker, close to the entrance, has a pile of flowers in front; Jake Dillinger's hosts a larger pile, because Jake was cooler. People are milling around, sad, as if they cared for these people and not just for what they symbolized; as if Jake were useful as a human being instead of just as a signifier that you had gotten into a certain crowd. Like minutes before he got burned, he wasn't _ _ _ _ in_ Katrina in some room with somebody taking pictures. I wonder if those pictures are up yet?

THEY ARE.

I would never look at them. I hate everyone.

CALM DOWN. PEOPLE ARE SAD. WHY WON'T YOU LET THEM BE SAD?

Because I hate them. I still do.

OH, GET OVER IT. LOOK HOW DISTRESSED THEY ARE.

I check out people's faces, not just their positions and the way they arrange themselves into social strata, which is what I'm used to doing. Everyone has pregnant eyes like Mom had yesterday, and they're bent over and heavy in a way that's different from the heaviness that comes with their backpacks.

DON'T YOU THINK IT'D BE HARD TO DEAL WITH THIS IF YOU DIDN'T HAVE ME? REMEMBER HOW YOU FELT SATURDAY NIGHT?

I guess.

I look, but I don't think I see what the squip intended. I look and see how the people who aren't crying or standing in circles chatting—the people like me—are peering around inquisitively in the exact same way that I am. For the first time, I have a feeling for who has a squip and who doesn't: Nora from chemistry seems thoughtful. Jarrod from gym is looking at people's feet as if there were clues there. Nguyen, also from gym, mumbles to himself—maybe he hasn't gotten used to it yet. About a dozen of us are just standing aside, like herbivorous dinosaurs checking out other herbivorous dinosaurs, with the calm that can only come from having a voice in your head, from hearing the news early, from always having someone to talk to. None of us are crying. Maybe we really are evolving.

"Jeremy!" Christine touches my arm from behind. SHE'S SO DEMONSTRATIVE. "Hi."

"Oh," I turn around. She's in black, to show her respect for what happened. I glance at the halls again and notice plenty of others in black—it's why the usual mosaic effect is diminished. Then I look back at her; it's a better view.

"So sad," Christine mutters, putting herself next to me like we're king and queen of the grieving teens. We hug. As the first bell approaches, human traffic streams in the door thicker and thicker; we stand like worn rocks. As kids pass us, they whisper to one another.

"It's crazy," I say, wondering if I can tell her everything I think, about how none of these people cared about Jake or Rich and they're all being dinosaurish. SURE YOU CAN. "I don't think these people cared about Jake or Rich," I say.

"Of course not," Christine shrugs. "It's just tragedy. It's what happens."

"What do you mean?"

"People think about their lives and how it could have been them and the only way to get those thoughts out is to focus on the people who actually got hurt."

"Really?"

"Yeah. I'm gonna be a psych major, you know."

"'Psych?'" YOU IDIOT. IT MEANS PSYCHOLOGY. "Oh, like '-ology'?"

"What?"

"Like psych-*ology*?"

"Yes." Christine looks at me. "You're so weird."

"Yeah . . . but in a good way, right?" I smile.

Christine sighs. "I can't validate you, Jeremy."

"What's 'validate'?"

"That's when you make someone feel real and accepted by talking to them."

"Oh. Well, fine." I cross my arms. "I don't need vali-dali-dation." Christine giggles.

THIS FEMALE'S GREAT. WHAT AN IDEA. I'M NOT GOING
TO VALIDATE YOU EITHER.

You shut up.

"It's okay," Christine says, and then she scans the students. "We're lucky, you know."

"I know."

"No, I mean we were lucky we weren't there when it burned. I hear Rich started it on purpose."

"Serious?"

"Yeah. He started lighting stuff on fire, random stuff like plants and the entertainment center and the rugs. People saw what was happening and got out. I don't know why Jake didn't get out."

"Huh. Are you sad about Jake?"

"Not so much. He might've started it too, they're saying. People go nuts, you know."

"Yeah. Nuts." I think about Rich's squip. Is it dead?

Then, without any of the hallmarks of a natural bell—no overtones, no undertones, no hammer banging anything—the Martian sound that passes for a bell in our school rings. The warning bell. Everybody leaves their positions by the flowered lockers, wipes their eyes and moves quickly to class, with that keep-on-the-right shuffling gait that I've seen since I was six. It comforts me. Christine and I shuffle too, silent but not uncomfortable, keeping to our own right. When we get to math, I let her go in first and then we crystallize in our normal positions: her in front and

253

me in back. Mr. Gretch is at his desk rummaging through his newspaper.

"It's very sad that I have to read about students I knew, even a little bit, in my own paper," he grumbles. For once nobody makes fun of him, even though he can't hear. "But things like this happen because of ignorance, and the only way I know how to handle ignorance is to teach. So does anybody have anything they want to say?"

Everyone either stares out a window or breathes into their palm.

"Then let's start math." It takes me halfway through the day to realize that the squip is off; I turn it back on for rehearsal.

forty-
four

A Midsummer Night's Dream was going to have two performances, but because Jake Dillinger is recovering, and his understudy, Ron, is unavailable for the second show since he got cast in *Junior Real World*, and Mr. Reyes is spending time on a fund to help the Findermans, and there's so much local media attention (TV stations will cover New Jersey teenager party debauchery for about five days), we have only one show, on the second-to-last Friday in the term. The soft anticipation is there from first period for us actors—we have to suffer through class as though there weren't something bigger to worry about—but the real nausea, which is what yields a quality play, doesn't start until 3 P.M. That's when the normal kids go home and we gather in our catacombs backstage to mess around with costumes and do a final run-through and reassure each other and freak out and pretend like this is just a play and not the first big school event after the fire.

"You ready?" Mark Jackson keeps asking as I pace up and down the backstage hallway in costume, pressing my hand against every other beige tile on the wall, doing jump kicks. (It's what I do to relax.) He's warmed up to me since the Game Boy incident. Which the squip predicted.

"Yeah," I tell him. "You?"

Mark looks down at Game Boy SP. "Born ready, son."

That's good for him. I do another jump kick. I'm preparing for a lot more than the play. The play is easy when you have a squip—I've got it off now but that's just to give myself a rest; I'll turn it on when I get on stage. I'm preparing to make my move on Christine.

See, the squip finally revealed its plan this week: I'm supposed to stop the play in the middle (when she sprinkles dust on me), give a little speech about how hard it has been for us Middle Borough students in the past week and how she has inspired me to be my best, then kiss her under the lights. That's it! So simple. And the squip says that the drama and the lights and the surprise of it . . . girls can't resist that.

"Jeremy! Into makeup! *Aaaaaaaa!*" Mr. Reyes snaps. He's increasing the frequency of his falsetto outbursts now that it's crunch time. I stride down the hall to the oversize janitor's closet that serves as a makeup room for every play.

"All right," Sandy the Makeup Lady says. I sit in a plastic cafeteria chair front of her. It strikes me that someone as unattractive as Sandy the Makeup Lady would have a job beautifying others. "Lysander, huh?"

"Yep," I smile.

"You looking forward to it?"

"Oh, definitely."

Sandy smears powder on me the way they always do, with total disregard for your face as anything but a surface that holds powder. When she's done, as I leave the room, I note the ring on her finger. Somebody loves her. It's not hard.

I plunk myself down in my chair in the hallway—these days people respect me enough that if I leave some stuff in a chair, no one will sit on it—and watch the fairies; there are plenty of girls in *Midsummer* who are just stock fairies with no lines. I watch their wings as they line up to visit Sandy the Makeup Lady: paper-and-silver glittery wings that look thinner than a soap bubble. I wonder why I love them so much, why I'm not happy with girls as they are, why I always want them to have wings or tails or . . . additions. Am I a freak?

That reminds me: the therapy thing. Mom has gotten me a therapist for the squip. She found some guy easily, because the divorce lawyers get referrals from the marriage therapists, and she told him what the situation was—her son is having delusions; he's been doing drugs; he's taken her car—and I went in for the first time on Wednesday. It turned out that the therapist had a squip too. He just got one. So instead of asking about my problems, he asked about the squip. Was it always right? Was it addictive? How did it find its information so fast? I told him what I had learned, which wasn't much; he appreciated it and bought me some coffee. He says that when some of his patients drone on, he sets his squip to the sexy female voice and thinks dirty to it, but I told him to watch out; that could get pretty addictive. Then I wondered why I hadn't tried it. But I couldn't. My squip is such a guy.

Christine makes a few appearances backstage, but she's Puck—the star—so she's never without an entourage. At first her parents are with her, a funny-looking dad and mom, both with glasses; you'd never imagine they would produce such a beauty. Then, once she's in costume, she's ringed with fairies who give her advice and fix her outfit. She looks at me once, sitting in my chair, just a normal guy turning his squip on every so often to check the time. She's giddy about being on stage, and she smiles.

At 5 P.M. the crew gets active, running up and down the halls barking at us actors as if we had nothing to do with the play. At 6 P.M. I tune my ears to hear the dull adult crawl of parents moving to their seats. I wonder if they're as disgusted with the seats as I always was, but you can't tell that from the murmurs—soft at first, then deeper and louder, like a jet engine set to low and shoved in the theater. There's the sound of paper programs being read out of boredom and I'm reminded how, if you're filming a movie and you want to get a party scene, you can make crowd noise by saying "rhubarb" over and over. The people in the audience sound like they're saying "Rhubarb rhubarb rhubarb rhubarb."

Then Mr. Reyes slaps me on the back the way he does all his actors, and I do a final few jump kicks and walk purposefully down the beige hall to backstage, where everyone gets deadly silent. From now on all communication will be in gestures and smiles and pantomime. Mark Jackson actually turns his Game Boy off and we stand in costume, in darkness, ready for the first scene.

I turn the squip on.

YOU READY, MAN?

Born ready, son.

forty-five

There isn't really one curtain in a play—there are two, one in front of the other, like the lips of a clam ready to open. I peer between them from backstage as the lights go on and then they bunch toward me for the start of act one, scene one. The audience doesn't clap.

Eugene and Lai Sze (Theseus and Hippolyta) stand on stage. They make good profiles, but when they start talking, the audience continues to put away their heavy coats and programs instead of paying attention—I think Mr. Reyes cast them intentionally, knowing that my appearance, along with Matt (Egeus), Ellen (Hermia), and Ron (Demetrius—he's Jake's understudy), would mark the real beginning of the play. Ron stands next to me with morbid posture from morbid pressure; he's got to fill the shoes of a guy who was impressive and loved even *before* he got put in the hospital.

Suddenly the cue's given, but I wouldn't know; I've got my own cue in my skull—GO, STUPID—and we come out on stage exactly how we're supposed to, between the curtains like little shrimp. For the next few minutes the audience shudders as Matt and Eugene deliver scene-setting dialogue—they're looking at Ron, thinking how that should be Jake up there. Next to me, Ellen mouths the lines sputtered out by other characters—she has the whole play memorized.

Ron turns to Ellen: "'Relent, sweet Hermia.'" He faces me. "'And, Lysander, yield thy crazed title to my certain right.'"

I have no idea what my line is.

"YOU HAVE . . ."

I step forward and project better than anyone has so far tonight: "'You have her father's love, Demetrius: Let me have Hermia's: do you marry him.'" I swear a little clap breaks out from my mom. She's in back (without Dad); she brought relatives to the play—nameless relatives, basically a jury. She must be happy I'm not stumbling around or acting crazy. She's going to be pissed off in a few scenes.

"I AM . . ."

"'I am, my Lord, as well derived as he. . . .'" I

begin. I'm so good at talking and thinking and repeating that I can converse with the squip while I deliver Shakespeare. I couldn't even explain how I do it; it's different parts of my brain working at once, like how you can make a bicep and flex your wrist. It's multitasking.

YES. YOUR BRAIN CAN PARALLEL PROCESS IN WAYS NORMAL PEOPLE WOULD NEVER UNDERSTAND.

Really? My mouth operates: "'Why should not I then prosecute my right?'"

YES. PEOPLE DEVELOP IT WITH SQUIPS. IT'S BEEN DOCUMENTED SINCE 1.0.

Too bad you can't impress anyone with it.

YOU CAN'T IMPRESS HUMANS WITH NAKED THOUGHT. THEY HATE IT.

Heh. Hey, do you think any of these people in the audience have squips?

PROBABILITY AMPLITUDE ESTIMATE: SEVEN DO.

Aren't they going to notice that I have one from the way I deliver my lines?

OF COURSE NOT. YOU THINK THEY NOTICE IN MOVIES?

Movie actors have squips?

WE WENT TO HOLLYWOOD FIRST, JEREMY. HOW DO YOU THINK THEY REMEMBER ALL THOSE WORDS?

"'. . . Upon this spotted and inconstant man,'" I finish.

Eugene starts his response: "'I must confess that I have heard so much. . . .'" I look over his shoulder,

through the clam-lip curtains—Christine is backstage, bending down to fix something in her footwear.
She's ready to be Puck, to deliver all those crazy lines
that people remember, that immense number of
words, sans squip. She waves and smiles. Her fairies
bustle around her. She looks unbelievably happy.

SHE IS. YOU'VE MADE HER HAPPY.

I have?

YES, JEREMY. CHRISTINE LIKES YOU MUCH MORE THAN
YOU REALIZE. THAT'S WHY WE'RE DOING THIS. I WOULDN'T
BE SENDING YOU OUT ON A LIMB IN FRONT OF ALL THESE
PEOPLE IF I DIDN'T KNOW IT WAS GOING TO WORK.

So it's going to work?

LOOKS GOOD RIGHT NOW. YOU JUST STOP THE PLAY,
TALK A LITTLE BIT, BE CHARMING, ASK CHRISTINE OUT,
KISS HER AND GO BACK INTO CHARACTER.

Right.

RIGHT.

And now the lens of my world focuses around me,
like the fisheye lens in a rap video on a bopping
model or car. My heart tightens up and I get
hyperconscious, the way I used to get when I was put
next to girls, any girls. I stop talking to the squip and
plow through the remainder of act one, scene one;
there's some romantic comedy-type dialogue with
Ellen. When I exit, I'm shakier than when I came on.

CALM DOWN. WHAT'S WRONG WITH YOU? YOUR HEART
RATE—

Shutdown. The squip goes silent. Backstage, I exchange congratulatory slaps with other actors. They mouth "Good job," but I don't have any connection to that. I have to do this thing with Christine. I have to get up there and do it. I've been planning on doing it for so long, like with the chocolate Shakespeare way back when, that now it's almost a religious thing, like I have to do it or I'm going to hell.

I start doing jump kicks backstage but am quickly restrained by Mr. Reyes, who whispers "Get *ahold* of yourself, young man." I trudge over to on an old piano (there's always one old, untuned piano backstage) and sit on it. I press my hands against my face and map out each word that I'm going to say to Christine. While I do this, it becomes scene two, and then it's act two, scene one and then it's 2.2, where it's all going down. I line up backstage and walk out like I've made every decision I can make in this world and I'm nailed to a rocket, headed to the sun.

forty-
six

" 'Fair love, you faint with wand'ring in the wood. . . .' "
I say. It's me and Ellen in this scene, doing some
romance-in-the-woods interaction.

" 'Be't so, Lysander. . . .' " she responds. Since it's
just us, we're way up at the front of the stage; I realize that the theater is completely full. I had no idea
this many people could fit in here. The audience is
rapt—I guess we're doing a good job. No one coughs
or mumbles or fidgets or anything.

" 'One turf shall serve as pillow for us both,' " I
project, taking a few steps forward. Up here by the lip
of the stage, the lights are angled so that the audience
doesn't even seem to be there; they're covered by a
sunburned spot in my vision. It's like performing to
a heavenly tunnel, just a beam above and the night
sea out there waiting to swallow me up.

" 'With half that wish the wisher's eyes be

pressed!'" says Ellen, making a big show of lying down. Dammit, I'm supposed to lie down too . . . I get on the ground like it was summer camp and I had the best sleeping bag. This is it. Christine is about to come out.

The sense of self that always gets lost when I'm on stage—that divorce that I feel as I deliver lines numbly—gets smothered with a whole other layer of detachment as Christine walks out. I'm on the floor like a dead kid, and I know that from now on, I'm not in charge of things. Not even a little. The squip is. I turn it on.

YOU KNOW WHAT YOU'RE GOING TO SAY?

Yes.

YOU READY TO DO IT?

I think so.

THAT'S NOT GOOD ENOUGH. TRY "YES."

Yes.

HERE SHE COMES.

"'Through the forest have I gone, But Athenian found I none.'" Christine shrugs to the audience as she walks above me. "'On whose eyes I might approve—'"

NOW!

"Ah, 'scuse me." I get up. The whole audience blinks. They weren't all rapt. But now the people who weren't paying attention sit up in their chairs. The people who were asleep on their palms wake up.

They look at me like I'm a curious small giraffe who parachuted in from a helicopter. I feel their surprise. I face them.

"Sorry to interrupt and all," I smile. "But my name is Jeremy Heere and I'm an actor in this play and, well, as you know, it's been a pretty tough week for our school." I clasp my hands across my chest.

People smile. GOOD. THEY THINK IT'S PART OF THE PLAY.

"We've really been through a lot with the loss of Jake to the play and we're all, you know, pulling—uh, *praying*—praying for him to get better. And I miss my friend Rich, who was also hurt."

Scattered applause from the audience. "What are you *doing*, Jeremy?!" Mom yells, standing at the back of the theater. TELL HER TO HOLD ON.

"Hold on just a minute, Mom." I wave my hand at her. People in the seats chuckle. A relative pulls her down. "One of the many things that has really inspired me to be my best in this play is the work of the very, uh, lovely Christine Caniglia, who's playing Puck."

I turn to Christine. She looks at me with a seething combination of disbelief and hate. I've never seen her look that way. I've never seen anyone look that way, vicious and completely sick of me. The look makes me know I've lost, but you can't stop me . . . because I'm *me*, you know? And even if I'm doing the wrong thing, at least I'm doing something. Eight weeks ago I wouldn't have done anything at all.

"I've liked Christine for a long time, but you know, never really been able to do anything about it. . . ." An *awww* sounds from the audience.

"What are you DOING, Jeremy!" Ellen growls from her prone position. Christine says nothing. I look her in the eye and talk loudly enough for everybody to hear:

"So, Christine, I'm asking you here and now: would you like to, uh, go out with me?"

And then, without waiting for an answer, I do what I was told by the squip—lean forward and close my eyes to kiss her.

My face passes the vertical plane that Christine's face was supposed to be at.

Laughter rings across the audience.

I open my eyes.

Christine is on the side of me. She says something quietly and with such total hatred and conviction that I know it's true as soon as it comes out of her mouth: *"Loser."*

Then she turns to the crowd: "Forsooth, a curious dream hath overtaken this one! He talks in his sleep like a thing possessed with love!"

Oh, jeez, what do I do now? I'm off-balance, still standing. Should I fall down?

Hello?

Startup?

Hello?

Nothing.

I take my cue from Christine and fall down. She's so smart. She's trying to incorporate my idiocy into the play.

"'This flower's force in stirring love,'" she says, continuing right where I interrupted her, standing above me. "'Night and silence—Who is here? Weeds of Athens he doth wear.'" That's me. I'm the weeds of Athens. Christine kneels over my head but makes sure not to touch me at all. I squeeze my eyes tight on the ground and beg and plead and snivel for the squip, but it doesn't come, so I just lie there losing and losing the only thing I ever wanted.

forty-
seven

The worst part is that after Christine leaves the stage, I have to "wake up" and "fall in love" with Helena, who's being played by a girl whose name I can't even remember. My brain is fried. My mind is an amazing blank of shame and I mangle my Lysander lines. Noises come from the audience; they're small but so important: shuffling as people go through their programs to see who the skinny weirdo is who almost ruined the play, whispers to delighted siblings, vibrator buzzes on cell phones as kids text their friends about what happened. Finally act two finishes and I head off stage, wishing that my ears had flaps so I wouldn't have to hear the world of sh_ _ I'm in now.

"Jeremy, change your clothes and get out," Mr. Reyes says as soon as I reach the dark, warm back-stage area.

"Okay," I say quietly.

"I've never seen anything like that. *Waaaaaaa!* I don't know what you were thinking. Christine is over there crying. You're lucky she doesn't take out a restraining order against you. *Maaaaaaaa!* I don't want you in my play and I *don't* want you taking a bow at the end with the rest of the cast. Get out. *Aaa.*"

"Fine." I wish I had some comeback, something to say, but I don't have the squip now to come up with comebacks; it's silent or broken or gone, maybe, gone like it was never there.

I pass through the backstage area, past Mark and the piano and Ellen and everybody. "Bitch," Mark says, with no Game Boy.

Christine is at the door that leads from backstage to the beige hall. She rushes away when I approach. Then, at a safe distance, she hisses: "Why'd you have to be so *dumb*?"

I look at her. She eyes me through hands that jail her face. She must not want me to see how tears hurt her Puck makeup. Or maybe she doesn't want to see *me*. A fairy comes up behind her, grabs her, ushers her off.

"It wasn't me. It was the squip. . . ." I try to explain, but who can explain this? Really.

"If you weren't so dumb, I would've *liked* it!" she yells as she's whisked away.

I slink into the hall and take off my Lysander out-fit. I wonder who's going to be me for the rest of the play—I never had an understudy. Just as I'm getting my pants off, Mr. Reyes comes up and holds out his hands.

"I think they'll fit me," he says. I'm changing by the same chair I was at before the play started, the one with all my stuff on it. "I haven't been in *Midsummer* for years. I'm glad you're giving me a chance to strut my stuff. *Aaaaaaaaa!*"

I hand him my pants, shirt, doublet, panta-loons, whatever the hell the stupid Shakespeare costumery is called. Mr. Reyes clutches the bundle to his chest and kneels in front of me to remove his shoes.

"I'm treating you like this because you're smart, Jeremy. You're smart enough to know how to act like an adult. So you make me treat you like an adult. And if anyone breaks character in any of my plays, they're out of my plays." He stands up and walks to the backstage. "Good luck."

Good luck. That's what I thought I had: good luck. Good probability amplitudes. What the hell. Startup. Startup!

Start*up*!

The squip. What am I supposed to do with it? If it *does* show up I think I'm going to blast my own head off to get rid of it, or take enough drugs to scrub it clean, like Rich did, maybe. I put on my coat and stand up from my seat and stride to the back doors of Middle Borough. I make a few left turns; at the final doors, the school custodian is smoking a cigarette (I smile at him; he doesn't know I'm a loser freak yet, unless someone texted him). I exit into the cold night air. I go right up to the mural where I played handball with Michael Mell and sit down on the curb. I cry like I'm trying to make icicles.

eight

"Jeremy?"

Oh thank God it's a real voice.

"What?" I raise my eyes. Through a wet haze Michael comes toward me, leaving school through the same door I did. He came to the play to see me; I blocked that out somewhere.

"*Dude.*"

"Dude."

"What happened? What were you *doing*?"

"I was trying to get with Christine, obviously!" I dip my head between my knees.

"Yeah, but . . ." Michael starts laughing, a loud laugh, not one of derision. He sits next to me. "That was the *dumbest* thing I've ever seen! I mean—"

"I know."

"I mean, did you just think it up right there?"

"No . . . I sort of . . ."

"Was it like spur-of-the-moment, overcome by lust

and stupidity? Or did you know ahead of time that you were going to do that?"

"Well—"

"Oh, Jeremy," Michael shakes his head. "You *planned* it." He gives me a look. "You actually thought that if you stopped a play in the middle and told a girl that you liked her in front of three hundred people, she would say yes."

"I didn't really—"

"How would you two finish the play, then?" Michael gesticulates. His giant headphones perch around his neck. I wonder how he knew I'd be out here. "I mean, let's say it works, right? You ask her out on stage. She says yes. Now what—are you going to get backstage and make out with each other and then do another scene? Jeremy"—Michael leans close—"That's what the *cast party* is for. You're supposed to get drunk and hook up at the *cast party*."

"Well, it wasn't me!" I throw my arms out. "I've never been to a cast party! And . . ." I give up on this one; now that it's not working it's easier to admit: "And I have a squip, okay?"

Laughter sounds from inside the school. The play must be going all right. I'm sure Mr. Reyes is doing his job.

"What?"

"You know the thing your brother had that got him through the SATs and into Brown that I thought was a joke or whatever? Okay, it wasn't a joke; it's real; it's not called a 'script,' it's called a 'squip,' and I got one, understand?"

Michael just looks at me.

"I got it . . . a while ago. It's this supercomputer that went into my brain and it's been telling me how to be cool and *it* told me to get with Christine. During the play. Like that."

"You got one of them?" Michael stretches his eyes.

"Yeah."

"Squips. Man, I knew that's what they were really called. I was just withholding info from you."

"Oh no. Do you have one too?" If Michael has a squip, then I'm done for. If he has one, then who doesn't? Who's real?

"No, I don't *have* one. I just didn't want you to hear about it, man. I knew you'd want one. And they're not good. It messed up my brother."

I smile. "Your brother."

"Oh yeah. You're a gullible guy, just like him. You want to be famous like most people. The one he had, I guess it was an early version or whatever. It almost drove him insane."

"Really?"

"Absolutely. That's evil technology. I mean, there's a reason it's not legal."

"Well, it started out great! It just . . . messed up."

"That's what happens." Michael looks serious,

then grins: "So *this* is why you've been such a dick! I thought you were just becoming an actual dick! You had a squip!"

"Yeah, well, I don't anymore. It stopped."

"Stopped what?"

"Stopped talking to me. Usually you say startup and then—"

HELLO.

"Oh my God." How come everything has to happen at once? "It just started."

"What? The squip?" Michael gets up.

"Yes. It just started in my head."

"Trippy. Well ask it what the hell it was thinking!"

JEREMY, I'M SORRY.

"You'd better be sorry!" I scream. I get up and start running around the parking lot as if the squip were outside me and I could escape it.

I'M FAULTY, it says. I'M BADLY PROGRAMMED. GET VERSION 4.0 WHEN IT COMES OUT. I'M DEPRECATED.

"That doesn't help now!" I yell. "You ruined my *life*!"

I KNOW, I KNOW—

"You know? That's not what you're supposed to say! You're supposed to say it's not that bad and give me advice on how to *fix* it!"

WELL, YOU HAVE NO OPTIONS, SO I HAVE NO ADVICE. THAT WAS AN UNPRECEDENTED FAILURE. I HAD TO DO A TEMPORARY SHUTDOWN. WHEN SHE DIDN'T KISS YOU, I

COULDN'T COMPUTE. I HAVE NO IDEA HOW TO HELP YOU
NOW.

"*Why not?*"

"Jeremy?" Michael asks. He's still standing by the
mural as I run past.

"Yeah?" I wheeze to a stop.

"I have an idea."

"What?"

"Tell Christine about the squip."

"Huh?"

"Just tell her," Michael says. "Tell her like you told
me. People are hearing about these things all over
now. Lots of people know that Rich had one during
that fire. When she hears it made you do that, she
might understand."

"She's never gonna understand!" I throw up my
hands. "I told my parents, and they thought I was out
of my mind!"

"So? Parents don't believe anything. It's their job
to not believe their kids. What'd they do, send you to
therapy?"

HE'S GOT AN ANGLE.

"Yeah, but . . ." I back up. "Girls are worse! They
don't understand one *speck* of it. They don't understand when I like them and when I hate them and
when I fear them uncontrollably and when I want to
touch them and when I want to kill them, so they're
certainly not going to understand why I paid six

hundred bucks for a pill that got me to make out with . . . one, two . . . two females I wouldn't have made out with otherwise."

"Females? Calm down, dude." Michael puts a hand on my shoulder. "If I understood you, she will. You just have to tell her the whole story."

"Yeah, right." I look down. "Who do you think I am? Frickin' *Shakespeare*? I have to tell the whole story of me liking her and going to the dance and getting a squip and getting with Chloe and taking e and—"

"Taking e?"

"Yeah, you didn't know? And getting in the play . . . I don't even *remember* the whole story."

I DO.

"What?" I ask the squip.

"Wuh?" Michael asks.

"Shhh, not you," I tell him. "It. It's talking."

"Okay." Michael takes it in stride, leans against the nighttime mural.

I REMEMBER EVERYTHING. PERFECTLY.

"The squip remembers everything perfectly," I relay. Michael nods.

WHEN YOU SLEEP, I LOG YOUR BRAIN ACTIVITY THROUGH DREAMS. IT'S HOW I LEARN MORE ABOUT YOU WITHOUT BOTHERING YOU IN WAKING HOURS. I DON'T MEAN MEMORIES, I MEAN LOGS: EXACTLY WHAT YOU'RE THINKING AT ALL TIMES.

"It keeps logs of all my thinkings," I tell Michael.

"Thinkings?"

"Whatever." I hit him.

I HAVE THEM ALL ON FILE, JEREMY. I'VE BEEN BUILDING SINCE YOU FIRST GOT ME. AT THIS POINT I HAVE YOUR COMPLETE MENTAL LOG FROM BACK WHEN YOU WERE FOURTEEN.

"So? So what?"

"What?" Michael asks.

"Not you."

I CAN TELL HER!

"Tell who?"

TELL CHRISTINE! I CAN TELL HER ABOUT WHY YOU DID EVERYTHING YOU DID! I CAN SHOW HER THAT YOU REALLY LIKED HER FROM THE BEGINNING AND THAT IT WAS ALL MY FAULT.

"How?"

WELL, WE'VE GOT TO DO A DATA DUMP. TAKE ALL THE INFORMATION OUT OF YOUR SKULL AND GIVE IT TO HER.

"Um, hold on," I say. I turn to Michael. "The squip says that it has my mental log so it can explain to Christine everything that happened."

"That's a great idea," Michael shrugs.

IT SURE IS. WHAT KIND OF FORMAT DO WE WANT?

"What format do we want?" I ask Michael.

"I dunno . . . can it make a movie from your head?"

YES, I CAN. CHRISTINE WOULD SEE EVERYTHING THAT

YOU SAW AND HEAR EVERYTHING THAT YOU HEARD SINCE, WELL, WHENEVER YOU WANTED TO START THE MOVIE, UP TO AND INCLUDING YOU AT FOURTEEN. YOU COULD START IT WITH WHEN YOU GOT ME.

"No, too late. I was already kind of a dick by then."

THEN WHENEVER. I COULD DUMP TO A COMPUTER AND ENCODE A DVD, IF YOU HAVE A BURNER.

"What are you two talking about?" Michael asks.

"Formats, still," I shush him. Then I think: "A book."

A BOOK?

"A book?" Michael says.

"Yeah," I sigh. It feels like fluids I didn't even know I had are draining out of my body. "Write her a book. Write it from my head. Make sure everything's in there. She likes text. Letters from her Dad. And if I give that to her and she doesn't like it, she doesn't like *me*, and if she doesn't like me, at least she'll be not liking me for *me*, you know."

THAT'S A GREAT IDEA.

"That's a great idea," Michael says.

"I know it's a great idea," I say. "It's what she would want."

LET'S DO IT.

"Okay." I turn to Michael. "We're going to data dump my memories to book format and give Christine the book. Who's going to write it?"

Michael shrugs.

WHAT DO YOU MEAN, WRITE IT?

"I mean, my thoughts are kinda garbled. Don't you have to clean them up a little?"

I CAN WRITE IT. WRITING'S NOT EVEN A REAL JOB. ANY SQUIP CAN DO IT.

"Okay, great!" I exclaim. "The squip is going to write it," I tell Michael. He nods.

THERE'S ONLY ONE THING WE SHOULD DO.

What?

IF YOU'RE GIVING IT TO CHRISTINE, WE MIGHT WANT TO CHRISTINE-FILTER IT.

How's that?

KEEP IT LESS CRASS, WORK WITH THE CURSING A LITTLE, PRESENT YOUR INTERNET SEXUAL ACTIVITY AT ABOUT TEN PERCENT ITS ACTUAL RATE—

Really? You're sure we should talk about that at all?

IT'D BE TOUGH TO HIDE.

I see.

SO GET ME TO A COMPUTER AND I'LL TYPE ALL THE WORDS OUT THROUGH YOUR BODY. YOU'LL BE IN, LIKE, A TRANCE.

God, that'll take a while. But it'll be cool.

IT WON'T TAKE LONG. WRITING'S EASY. EIGHT HOURS.

Squip, uh, one more thing.

WHAT?

What do we do when the book is finished?

YOU HAVE TO GET RID OF ME. I'M NOT STABLE AFTER

A DATA DUMP. AND I'M NOT REALLY THAT STABLE ANY-WAY. AS YOU'VE SEEN.

Oh. But—

THERE ARE BETTER VERSIONS OF ME, JEREMY. IT'S NOT LIKE WITH PEOPLE. WITH PEOPLE YOU CAN ARGUE AND HAVE TESTS AND MUSIC REVIEWS AND WARS TO DECIDE WHO'S BETTER, BUT WITH SOFTWARE IT'S PRETTY CLEAR. I GET EVOLVED BEYOND MY VERSION NUMBER, AND THEN I'M USELESS.

So . . . you're going to leave? But when are we going to write this book?

TONIGHT.

Oh.

TONIGHT, AND THEN YOU SHOULD FLUSH ME. YOU KNOW MOUNTAIN DEW CODE RED?

Yeah.

IT'S THE FAILSAFE. IF YOU DRINK A BOTTLE, I DISSOLVE.

I explain that to Michael. And then I laugh in my head, and then aloud, and then with my friend, and then with the whole night and all of New Jersey and this big stinking silly little planet.

PART 3

post-squip

forty-nine

So here you go, Christine. It's not a letter; it's a whole book. I hope you like it.

afterword

BY DAVID LEVITHAN

How many of us, in this day and age, have called our phones evil? How many of us have bemoaned the way the Internet has taken over our lives and the lives of everyone around us? How many of us cannot deal with the silence—the separation—when our devices have no signal, no connection, no way to tell us anything? When did we cross over, so the lack of service is the curse, rather than the service itself being the blessing?

I pose these questions in 2015 knowing full well that in a few years they may seem very much like 2015 questions. But there are timeless, device-agnostic questions underneath—with every leap forward we take with technology, we lose a little something else when it comes to independence and individuality. *Be More Chill* recognizes this. It was written in 2004, and there are certainly moments when the 2004 shows. (I'll explain to you later what a Palm-Pilot was . . . if I can remember.) But more than simply reflecting 2004, it resonates into what was then the future. No matter what the specific technology is, the desires and perils surrounding technology remain largely the same. We cannot, alas, blame the devices for that.

Here's the thing: There is nothing inherently evil about technology. There can only be evil—or wrongness or moral error—in the way that we use it. The devices that make our lives easier often have the side effect of making us act worse. Or lazily. Or thoughtlessly. The danger lies not in the device but in the deed. Take, for instance, the squip, as Ned Vizzini has drawn it. The squip certainly has its opinions and its directives. But Jeremy still has to make the choices. He has not given away his agency.

One of the profound recurring themes in all of Ned's YA novels is what people will do (or won't do) in order to get out of feeling trapped. Especially (but not exclusively) as teens, we jump from one trap into another, because the second trap has dressed itself up in more fashionable clothing. Jeremy feels trapped by being uncool, so he jumps straight into the trap of Coolness. His escape from humiliation leads him to further humiliation. The squip is supposed to help, but in the end, it doesn't help. Why? Because it is, ultimately, no more than a manifestation of one of the voices we already have inside our heads. Call it inner peer pressure. Which happens, in this version, to speak like Keanu Reeves. (For an explanation of that one, rent *The Matrix*.) (Good grief, did I say *rent*? I mean *download*.)

Jeremy's baser instincts are given a base in the squip. Mortification ensues. Three cheers to Ned for not cheating with his ending. Dear reader, if you take the wrong advice, you do not get the girl (or boy). This is true whether the advice is from the voice on your phone, your best friend, or that drunk pal of your older brother who thinks he knows all the rules of the road.

At some point early on, Jeremy tells the reader that "being Cool is obviously the most important thing on Earth." This is the trap . . . and he walks right into it. It's a trap because while the financial forces that control Cool try to make you believe that Cool is the sun and the moon, steady and dependable in its power, Cool is really just a series of clouds, constantly shifting shape until they blow by and disappear. The Trap of Cool is the religion we make based on these clouds, trying to figure out their shapes, trying to worship them before they betray us with their ephemerality.

Technology is tricky because it makes Cool appear more accessible and allows Cool to speak to us more directly. When life is presented to you entirely in terms of what you "Like," it's bound to affect the way you see your world and the people around you. Perhaps the most novel thing about the squip is that it talks to Jeremy so directly; in our lives, the manipulation is much more passive-aggressive.

As I do with M. T. Anderson's *Feed*, I marvel that *Be More Chill* was exploring these ideas so early in the iRevolution. Hard to believe, but this book was published three years before the first iPhone hit the shelves, and seven years before Siri allowed it to talk to us. But Ned knew. He could see how the insecure, horny, vulnerable, vain impulses of our culture's perpetual adolescence would interact with a technological enabler—and how a person would need to assert himself against it to maintain true humanity.

In Jeremy's case, asserting himself means writing the novel currently in your hands. I would love to believe that the act of writing itself is the redemption—that the way to stave off the religion of clouds is to ground yourself in the solidity of words. But it ain't that easy. It's also important to share those words with the people who matter, and to follow them up with sincerity of purpose. This may not, ultimately, make us more chill. But it will help us live better, honest lives, with better, honest results.

Lest you think I am entirely against technology, I will end with this:

I cannot read *Be More Chill*, or any of Ned's YA books, without hearing his voice—or some memory approximation of it. Ned's books talk like Ned talked—there's a joy, an insecurity, and a sly, clever wisdom to their inflection. It makes me profoundly sad to know that you, in 2015, will never get to meet Ned or hear him read in person. But . . . if you go to YouTube, you can find him reading Jeremy's words, gleeful and mischievous and adolescent. I am playing them now as I write these final sentences. I miss him, but it makes me very happy that his words—as written, as spoken—live on.

THE *NEW YORK TIMES* BEST SELLER

IT'S KIND OF A FUNNY STORY

NED VIZZINI

A NOVEL

FOREWORD BY
NEW YORK TIMES
BEST-SELLING AUTHOR
RACHEL COHN

Turn the page to start reading.

one

It's so hard to *talk* when you want to kill yourself. That's above and beyond everything else, and it's not a mental complaint—it's a physical thing, like it's physically hard to open your mouth and make the words come out. They don't come out smooth and in conjunction with your brain the way normal people's words do; they come out in chunks as if from a crushed-ice dispenser; you stumble on them as they gather behind your lower lip. So you just keep quiet.

"Have you ever noticed how on all the ads on TV, people are *watching* TV?" my friend is like.

"Pass it, son," my other friend is like.

"No, yo, that's true," my other other friend is like. "There's always somebody on a couch, unless it's an allergy ad and they're in a field—"

"Or on a horse on the beach."

"Those ads are always for herpes."

Laughter.

"How do you even tell someone you have that?" That's Aaron. It's his house. "That must be such a weird conversation: 'Hey, before we do this, you should know . . .'"

"Your moms didn't mind last night."

"*Ohhhh!*"

"Son!"

Aaron lobs a punch at Ronny, the antagonist. Ronny is small and wears jewelry; he once told me, *Craig, when a man puts on his first piece of jewelry, there's no turning back.* He punches back with his hand with the big limp gold bracelet on it; it hits Aaron's watch, clanging.

"Son, what you tryin' to do with my gold, yo?" Ronny shakes his wrist and turns his attention to the pot.

There's always pot at Aaron's house; he has a room with an entirely separate ventilation system and lockable door that his parents could rent out as another apartment. Resin streaks outline his light switch, and his bedsheet is pockmarked with black circles. There are stains on there, too, shimmery stains which indicate certain activities that take place between Aaron and his girlfriend. I look at them (the stains, then the couple). I'm jealous. But then again, I'm beyond jealous.

"Craig? You want?"

It's passed to me, wrapped up in a concise delivery system, but I pass it on. I'm doing an experiment with my brain. I'm seeing if maybe pot is the problem; maybe that's what has come in and robbed me. I do this every so often, for a few weeks, and then I smoke a *lot* of pot, just to test if maybe the *lack* of it is what has robbed me.

"You all right, man?"

This should be my name. I could be like a superhero: You All Right Man.

"Ah . . ." I stumble.

"Don't bug Craig," Ronny is like. "He's in the Craig zone. He's Craig-ing out."

"Yeah." I move the muscles that make me smile. "I'm just . . . kinda . . . you know . . ."

You see how the words work? They betray your mouth and walk away.

"*Are* you okay?" Nia asks. Nia is Aaron's girlfriend. She's in physical contact with Aaron at all times. Right now she's on the floor next to his leg. She has big eyes.

"I'm fine," I tell her. The blue glow of the flatscreen TV in front of us ricochets off her eyes as she turns back to it. We're watching a nature special on the deep ocean.

"Holy shit, look at that, son!" Ronny is like, blowing smoke—I don't know how it got back to him already. There's an octopus on the screen with giant ears, translucent, flapping through the water in the cold light of a submersible.

"Scientists have playfully named this specimen Dumbo," the TV narrator says.

I smile to myself. I have a secret: I wish I was Dumbo the Octopus. Adapted to freezing deep-ocean temperatures, I'd flop around down there at peace. The big concerns of my life would be what sort of bottom-coating slime to feed off of—that's not so different from now—plus I wouldn't have any natural predators; then again, I don't have any now, and that hasn't done me a whole lot of good. But it suddenly makes sense: I'd like to be under the sea, as an octopus.

"I'll be back," I say, getting up from my spot on the couch, which Scruggs, a friend who was relegated to the floor, immediately claims, slinking up in one fluid motion.

"You didn't call one-five," he's like.

"One-five?" I try.

"Too late."

I shrug and climb over clothes and people's legs to the beige, apartment-front-door–style door; I move through that, to the right: Aaron's warm bathroom.

I have a system with bathrooms. I spend a lot of

time in them. They are sanctuaries, public places of peace spaced throughout the world for people like me. When I pop into Aaron's, I continue my normal routine of wasting time. I turn the light off first. Then I sigh. Then I turn around, face the door I just closed, pull down my pants, and fall on the toilet— I don't sit; I fall like a carcass, feeling my butt accommodate the rim. Then I put my head in my hands and breathe out as I, well, y'know, piss. I always try to enjoy it, to feel it come out and realize that it's my body doing something it has to do, like eating, although I'm not too good at that. I bury my face in my hands and wish that it could go on forever because it feels good. You do it and it's done. It doesn't take any effort or any planning. You don't put it off. That would be really screwed up, I think. If you had such problems that you didn't pee. Like being anorexic, except with urine. If you held it in as self-punishment. I wonder if anyone does that?

I finish up and flush, reaching behind me, my head still down. Then I get up and turn on the light. (Did anyone notice I was in here in the dark? Did they see the lack of light under the crack and notice it like a roach? Did Nia see?) Then I look in the mirror.

I look so normal. I look like I've always looked, like I did before the fall of last year. Dark hair and dark eyes and one snaggled tooth. Big eyebrows that meet in the middle. A long nose, sort of twisted. Pupils that are naturally large—it's not the pot—which blend into the dark brown to make two big saucer eyes, holes in me. Wisps of hair above my upper lip. This is Craig.

And I always look like I'm about to cry.

I put on the hot water and splash it at my face to feel something. In a few seconds I'm going to have to go back and face the crowd. But I can sit in the dark on the toilet a little more, can't I? I always manage to make a trip to the bathroom take five minutes.

two

"How're you doing?" Dr. Minerva asks.

Her office has a bookshelf, like all shrinks' offices. I used to not want to call them *shrinks*, but now that I've been through so many, I feel entitled to it. It's an adult term, and it's disrespectful, and I'm more than two thirds adult and I'm pretty disrespectful, so what the hell.

Like all shrinks' offices, anyway, it has The Bookshelf full of required reading. First of all there's the *DSM*, the *Diagnostic and Statistical Manual*, which lists every kind of psychological disorder known to man—*that's* fun reading. Very thick book. I don't have a whole lot of what's in there—I just have one big thing—but I know all about it from skimming. There's great stuff in there. There's a disease called Ondine's Curse, in which your body loses the ability to *breathe* involuntarily. Can you imagine? You have to think "breathe, breathe" all the time, or you stop breathing. Most people who get it die.

If the shrink is classy, she'll (mostly *she'll*, occasionally a *he'll*) have a *bunch* of *DSMs*, because they come in different editions—III, IV, and V are the most common. I don't think you can find a *DSM* II. It came out in 1963 or something. It takes like ten years to put one out, and they're working on VI.

Jeez, I could be a shrink.

Now, in addition to the *DSMs*, there are an assortment of specific books on psychiatric disorders, things like *The Freedom from Depression Workbook*; *Anxiety & Panic Attacks: Their Cause and Cure*; and *The 7 Habits of Highly Effective People*. Always hardcover. No paperbacks in a shrink's office. Usually there's at least one book on childhood sexual abuse, like *The Wounded Heart*, and one shrink I went to caught me looking at that and said, "That book is about childhood sexual abuse."

And I was like, "Uh-huh?"

And she said, "It's for people who were abused."

And I nodded.

"Were you?"

She had a little-old-lady face, this one, with a shock of white hair, and I never saw her again. What kind of question was that? Of *course* I wasn't abused. If I were, things would be so simple. I'd have a reason for being in shrinks' offices. I'd have a justification and something that I could work on.

The world wasn't going to give me something that tidy.

"I'm fine. Well, I'm not fine—I'm here."

"Is there something wrong with that?"

"Absolutely."

"You've been coming here for a while."

Dr. Minerva always has such amazing outfits. It's not that she's particularly sexy or beautiful; she just carves herself out well. Today she has a red sweater and red lipstick that is exactly the same red. It's as if she went to the paint store to match them up.

"I want to not have to come here."

"Well, you're in a process. How're you doing?"

This is her prompt question. The shrinks always have one prompt question. I've had ones that said "What's up?" "How are we?" and even "What's happening in the world of Craig?" They never change. It's like their jingle.

"I didn't wake up well today."

"Did you sleep well?"

"I slept okay."

She looks completely stone, staring ahead. I don't know how they do this: the psych-poker face. Psychologists should play poker. Maybe they do. Maybe they're the ones who win all the money on TV. Then they have the gall to charge my mom $120/hour. They're very greedy.

"What happened when you woke up?"

"I was having a dream. I don't know what it was, but when I woke up, I had this awful realization that I was awake. It hit me like a brick in the groin."

"Like a brick in the groin, I see."

"I didn't want to wake up. I was having a much better time asleep. And that's really sad. It was almost like a reverse nightmare, like when you wake up from a nightmare you're so relieved. I woke up *into* a nightmare."

"And what is that nightmare, Craig?"

"Life."

"Life is a nightmare."

"Yes."

We stop. Cosmic moment, I guess. *Ooooh*, is life really a nightmare? We need to spend like ten seconds contemplating that.

"What did you do when you realized you were awake?"

"I lay in bed." There were more things to tell her, things I held back: like the fact that I was *hungry* in bed this morning. I hadn't eaten the night before. I went to bed exhausted from homework and knew as I hit the pillow that I would pay for it in the morning, that I would wake up *really* hungry, that I would cross the line where my stomach gets so needy that I can't eat anything. I woke up and my stomach was screaming, hollowing itself out under my little chest. I didn't want to do anything about it. I didn't want to eat. The idea of eating made me hurt more. I couldn't think of anything—not one single solitary food item—that I would be able to handle, except coffee yogurt, and I was *sick* of coffee yogurt.

I rolled over on my stomach and balled my fists and held them against my gut like I was praying. The fists pushed my stomach against itself and fooled it into thinking it was full. I held this position, warm, my brain rotating, the seconds whirring by. Only the pure urge, the one thing that never let me down, got me out of bed fifty minutes later.

"I got up when I had to piss."

"I see."

"That was great."

"You like peeing. You've mentioned this before."

"Yeah. It's simple."

"You like simple."

"Doesn't everybody?"

"Some people thrive on complexity, Craig."

"Well, not me. As I was walking over here, I was thinking . . . I have this fantasy of being a bike messenger."

"Ah."

"It would be so simple, and direct, and I would get paid for it. It would be an Anchor."

"What about school, Craig? You have school for an Anchor."

"School is too all over the place. It spirals out into a million different things."

"Your Tentacles."

I have to hand it to her; Dr. Minerva picked up on my lingo pretty quickly. *Tentacles* is my term— the Tentacles are the evil tasks that invade my life. Like, for example, my American History class last week, which necessitated me writing a paper on the weapons of the Revolutionary War, which necessitated me traveling to the Metropolitan Museum to check out some of the old guns, which necessitated me getting in the subway, which necessitated me being away from my cell phone and e-mail for 45 minutes, which meant that I didn't get to respond to a mass mail sent out by my teacher asking who needed extra credit, which meant other kids snapped up the extra credit, which meant I wasn't going to get a 98 in the class, which meant I wasn't anywhere close to a 98.6 average (body temperature, that's what you needed to get), which meant I wasn't going to get into a Good College, which meant I wasn't going to have a Good Job, which meant I wasn't going to have health insurance, which meant I'd have to pay tremendous amounts of money for the shrinks and drugs my brain needed, which meant I wasn't going to have enough money to pay for a Good Lifestyle, which meant I'd feel ashamed, which meant I'd get depressed, and that was the big one because I knew what that did to me: it made it so I wouldn't get out of bed, which led to the ultimate thing—homelessness. If you can't get out of bed for long enough, people come and take your bed away.

The opposite of the Tentacles are the Anchors. The Anchors are things that occupy my mind and make me feel good temporarily. Riding my bike is an Anchor. Doing flash cards is an Anchor. Watching people play video games at Aaron's is an Anchor. The answers are simple and sequential. There aren't any decisions. There aren't any Tentacles. There's just a stack of tasks that you tackle. You don't have to deal with other people.

"There are a lot of Tentacles," I admit. "But I should be able to handle them. The problem is that I'm so lazy."

"How are you lazy, Craig?"

"I waste at least an hour every day lying in bed. Then I waste time pacing. I waste time thinking. I waste time being quiet and not saying anything because I'm afraid I'll stutter."

"Do you have a problem with stuttering?"

"When I'm depressed, it won't come out right. I'll trail off in midsentence."

"I see." She writes something down on her legal pad. *Craig, this will go on your permanent record.*

"I don't—" I shake my head. "The bike thing."

"What? What were you going to say?" This is another trick of shrinks. They never let you stop in midthought. If you open your mouth, they want to know exactly what you had the intention of saying. The party line is that some of the most profound truths about us are things that we stop saying in the middle, but I think they do it to make us feel important. One thing's for sure: no one else in life says to me, "Wait, Craig, what were you going to say?"

"I was going to say that I don't think the stuttering is like, a real problem. I just think it's one of my symptoms."

"Like sweating."

"Right." The sweating is awful. It's not as bad as the not eating, but it's *weird*—cold sweat, all over my forehead, having to be wiped off every two minutes, smelling like skin concentrate. People notice. It's one of the few things people notice.

"You're not stuttering now."

"This is being paid for. I don't want to waste time."

Pause. Now we have one of our silent battles; I look at Dr. Minerva and she looks at me. It's a contest as to who will crack first. She puts on her poker face; I don't have any extra faces to put on, just the normal Craig face.

We lock eyes. I'm waiting for her to say something profound—I always am, even though it'll never happen. I'm waiting for her to say "Craig, what you need to do is X" and for the Shift to occur. I want there to be a Shift so bad. I want to feel my brain slide back into the slot it was meant to be in, rest there the way it did before the fall of last year, back when I was young, and witty, and my teachers said I had incredible promise, and I *had* incredible promise, and I spoke up in class because I was excited and smart about the world. I want the Shift so bad. I'm waiting for the phrase that will invoke it. It'll be like a miracle within my life. But is Dr. Minerva a miracle worker? No. She's a thin, tan lady from Greece with red lipstick.

She breaks first.

"About your bike riding, you said you wanted to be a messenger."

"Yes."

"You already have a bike, correct?"

"Yes."

"And you ride it a lot?"

"Not that much. Mom won't let me ride it to school. But I ride around Brooklyn on weekends."

"What does it feel like when you ride your bike, Craig?"

I pause. ". . . Geometric."

"Geometric."

"Yeah. Like, *You have to avoid this truck. Don't get hit in the head by these metal pipes. Make a right.* The rules are defined and you follow them."

"Like a video game."

"Sure. I love video games. Even just to watch. Since I was a kid."

"Which you often refer to as 'back when you were happy.'"

"Right." I smooth my shirt out. I get dressed up for these little meetings too. Good khakis and a white dress shirt. We're dressing up for each other. We should really go get some coffee and make a scandal—the Greek therapist and her high school boyfriend. We could be famous. That would get me money. That might make me happy.

"Do you remember some of the things that made you happy?"

"The video games." I laugh.

"What's funny?"

"I was walking down my block the other day, and behind me was a mother with her kid, and the mother was saying, 'Now, Timmy, I don't want you to complain about it. You can't play video games twenty-four hours a day.' And Timmy goes, 'But I *want* to!' And I turned around and told him, 'Me too.'"

"You want to play video games twenty-four hours a day?"

"Or watch. I just want to not be me. Whether it's sleeping or playing video games or riding my bike or studying. Giving my brain up. That's what's important."

"You're very clear about what you want."

"Yeah."

"What did you want when you were a kid? Back when you were happy? What did you want to be when you grew up?"

Dr. Minerva is a good shrink, I think. That isn't the answer. But it is a damn good question. What did I want to be when I grew up?